HILT'S PRIDE

A Bowl of Souls Novella

By

Trevor H. Cooley

The Bowl of Souls Series:

The Moonrat Saga

Book One: EYE of the MOONRAT

Book 1.5: HILT'S PRIDE

Book Two: MESSENGER of the DARK PROPHET

Book Three: HUNT of the BANDHAM

Book Four: The WAR of STARDEON

Book Five: MOTHER of the MOONRAT

The Jharro Grove Saga

Book Six: TARAH WOODBLADE

Book Seven: PROTECTOR of the GROVE

Book Eight: The OGRE APPRENTICE

HILT'S PRIDE

Trevor H. Cooley

Cover art by: Justin Cooley

Dedication

To my mother, Nancy Cooley. Thank you for all our late night talks. Thank you for being the one who for much of my life was my only friend and shoulder to cry on. Thank you for always supporting me and building me up. Thank you for being the one who taught me how to be able to laugh at myself, how to be kind to others, and perhaps most importantly for teaching me how to treat a woman.

Author's Note

The events in *Hilt's Pride* take place just after Hilt leaves Justan at the Training School part way through Bowl of Souls: Book One. This is a stand alone story and can be read apart from or along with the rest of the series. This story contains no spoilers to the rest of the series, but contains a lot of information that enhances the backgrounds of several characters.

When I first wrote about the character of Hilt so many years ago I was interested in his character and his history. At the time I intended to bring him back into the series, but he never seemed to fit into the direction the story went. Then nearly two years ago I had the idea to write a short story called *Hilt's Pride* and post it on my blog. I wrote the first two pages but never got around to finishing it.

After finishing book three of the Bowl of Souls, I knew that it would be a while until I could put out the fourth book and I wanted to put out something for my readers in the meantime. I had the idea to put together a series of short stories. *Hilt's Pride* was the first one that came to mind.

I had a vague outline in my head and figured the story would end up being around twenty to thirty pages. But as I started to write, the characters grew. I loved their interaction and humor and the tale of their journey grew in scope. I started telling people it would be sixty pages and before I knew it, I had realized it was going to be the size of a large novella.

I am very happy with the result and eager to share these characters with you. Please come to the Bowl of Souls Facebook page or message me on Twitter and tell me what you think. I hope you love the story as much as I do.

Trevor H. Cooley

Table of Contents

The Thunder People
Jack's Rest
Trafalgan Mountains
Academy
Reneul
Wobble
Pinewood
Dark Forest
Sampo
Silvertree Elves
Mage School
Tinny Woods
Fandine River
N
W
E
S
Wide River
Maloroo

I

The girl with the golden hair had come to die. It was the only answer that made sense. Hilt glanced back at the woman as the gorc's head hit the ground with a splash of dark blood.

She stood as if unafraid of the goblinoids that attacked. Her hair gleamed golden in the morning sunlight. Her eyes were fixed on him in curiosity, not in hope of rescue as he would expect.

Hilt stepped back from the dead creature as the next gorc attacked. He knocked aside its rusty iron blade. Stupid thing. It had to know it was outmatched. He had killed five of its comrades already. Hilt swept the tip of his left sword across its face, taking out an eye. It stumbled back with a howl, clutching at the wound. Hilt glared at the others, giving his swords a menacing twirl.

The two remaining gorcs grabbed their wounded comrade and retreated around a large nearby boulder, sending angry curses back at Hilt all the way. The fight seemed to be over, but Hilt knew that there were more gorcs nearby watching from the rocks.

Gorcs were little more than a nuisance to a trained warrior. They were a shade smaller than humans, larger and smarter than a lowly goblin, but smaller and stupider than an orc. Gorcs were in fact born from goblins, but gorcs despised their smaller brethren and formed tribes of their own.

Hilt didn't care where the creatures came from. They were mere rabble, unfit to stain his blade. He wouldn't have bothered if not for the girl.

He had first seen her earlier that morning climbing the steep incline of the mountainside alone. She had looked frail and vulnerable winding her way around the enormous boulders that littered the slope. Hilt had seen signs that the area was full of monsters and followed, intending to tell her to turn back. By the time he arrived, the gorcs had surrounded her.

Now that the immediate danger was over, Hilt turned to speak with her. But she was no longer standing there. The woman had turned back to the task of climbing the mountainside.

"Wait! Young lady!" Hilt caught up to her in moments. "Young lady, where are you going?"

"Young lady?"

She turned around and Hilt saw her up close for the first time. Now that she was out of the sunlight, her hair no longer gleamed golden. It was more of a dirtied blond. Her face was attractive, but weary. Her skin was tanned and wrinkled around piercing blue eyes. Her dress was long sleeved and woolen and quite dirty. This was a woman who spent most of her time outdoors, perhaps working the fields.

"I am surely no younger than you, swordsman." She turned back to climbing the steep slope. "Now leave me be. There are plenty more monsters for you to slay."

Hilt stared after her, blinking in disbelief. “Madam, I . . . I was not here to slay monsters. I was on a pressing mission when I saw the beasts surround you. I only followed you up here to keep you from getting killed!”

“Well you succeeded then. I am not dead.” she said, not looking back. “Now, if you’ll excuse me, I have my own ‘important duty’ to perform.”

He followed her up the slope a few moments more. “You truly aren’t going to thank me?”

“I never asked for your help, did I?” She took a few more labored strides up the mountainside, then paused and whirled around, her lips twisted into a scowl. “Just what were you expecting in thanks?”

"Expecting?" Hilt folded his arms across his chest. What an insolent woman. "When a man saves your life, isn't thanks customary?"

"Oh! So you followed me up here seeking a reward? Hmph, you sound like nobility." She eyed his clothing with suspicion. His garb was finely made but well worn and adjusted for easy movement. He wore leather boots, calf high with woolen breeches, and a white shirt covered by a chainmail vest and a fine overcoat. Sword sheathes hung at either hip and he had a small pack slung over his shoulders. "What did you want, a maiden's kiss of gratitude? Well I ain't no maiden!"

Hilt's face wrinkled in confusion. "Madam I most definitely did not come seeking a kiss."

She misunderstood the look on his face and gasped, one hand raising to her mouth. "A kiss not good enough? You see me, a baseborn woman all alone and think to take advantage? I think not. I may not be a maiden, but I'm not street trash! Go look for your 'thanks' elsewhere. I'll take my chances with the monsters!"

Hilt's face went red and he sputtered in outrage as she turned and resumed her climb. "Foul!" he cried finally.

She snorted and resumed her climb.

"That was a most- . . ." he strode quickly up the steep slope and passed the woman before turning to face her. "That was a most foul accusation! I climb up here out of my way to save your life and I am rewarded with scowls and disparaging remarks?"

"There you are expecting rewards again," she accused, taking a step backward. Her foot caught in her dress and she stumbled. She would have taken a tumble down the slope if Hilt had not reached out and grasped her arm. She struggled and slapped his arm as he pulled her to her feet. "Unhand me!"

Hilt made sure she had regained her footing before letting go, then raised both hands and took a step back. "I am sorry for my choice of words. I seek no reward. Truly. I just expected common courtesy is all."

Her blue-eyed glare softened only slightly. "Alright then,

you have your thanks. Now will you step aside, so I can get where I'm going?"

"I will not," Hilt said, arms folded, his voice firm.

Her fists clenched, but she forced a smile on her face. "Why thank you, kind sir. It was a privilege to be saved by a warrior such as yourself. There, is that better?"

Even though it was forced, Hilt had to admit her smile was pretty. He shrugged. "A bit better, yes."

"Then move it," she said, the smile still frozen on her face. She took a step forward, but Hilt did not move.

"I refuse," he said firmly.

Her eyes narrowed. "What do you want then?"

"Your safety," he replied. "No matter how mean tempered you are, I cannot in good conscience allow you to continue any farther. The way ahead would mean your certain death."

"And what makes you so sure?" she asked as her forced smile faded.

"For one, the gorcs are still watching us from the boulders below. More will likely join them and the only reason they haven't attacked us again already is the fact that I left six of them dead down there. Secondly, do you see these signs, my lady?" Hilt gestured to a small pile of stones next to her feet. They were white and irregularly shaped, but stacked evenly to form a small pyramid.

She nodded. "Rocks. What of it?"

"Look around you," he said, pointing to his right. Another similar pile of stones stood several yards away and she could see another one even further away. They seemed to be spaced apart evenly. "We crossed over similar signs earlier when we entered the gorc's territory."

She looked down at the piles and back up at him. "So we walked past piles of stones."

"You don't understand. The first signs we passed were made of plain stones set in a circular pattern. They are used to tell goblinoids when they're at the border of another tribe's territory.

The stones here, however, are stacked in a pyramid shape used by goblinoids to mark areas of danger. In other words, these stone represent a warning to their own tribe members to stay away."

"Good," she said. "That means they won't follow me up there. I hope you will follow their example."

Hilt grit his teeth in frustration. "Why are you so determined to die?"

"I won't die. At least I don't think so," she admitted, still seeming quite unconcerned. She tried to continue past him, but Hilt grabbed her shoulders with both hands, stopping her. She twisted and tore free from his grasp, nearly stumbling yet again. "Don't you touch me!"

"Then tell me."

"I will tell you nothing," she spat.

"I have half a mind to throw you over my shoulder and carry you down this mountain," Hilt said, his eyebrows raised at her ferocity.

"I would fight you the whole way!"

"You could not stop me. I could knock you unconscious if I had to. I would make sure you did not wake until I could take you to the nearest village and drop you off at an inn."

"I would have no choice in that case." Rage simmered behind her eyes, but she swallowed and gathered herself, then replied with complete calm. "However, if you did so, sir, I would only wait until you were gone and come back anyway."

"Be that as it may, I will do exactly as I threatened unless you tell me why you are so determined to ascend this mountain." Hilt said, jaw fixed in determination. "Tell me, woman, and do it fast because the gorcs are gathering in number."

Hilt pointed down the slope behind her. She turned to see that several more gorcs had joined the others and they were no longer bothering to hide. The one with the blinded eye was pointing up at them and snarling at the others. She looked back at Hilt and glared again.

"I can see that you are determined to continue, but do you

really want to be caught and likely eaten by those creatures?" Hilt prodded. "I will make you this concession. Tell me the truth and if your answer is satisfactory, not only will I let you go on, I will go down and slay the beasts just to give you a better chance."

She looked at Hilt's unmoving stance and up at the long climb ahead, then down to the gorcs below. When she looked back at him her expression was resigned. "Fine. Since you must know . . . the Prophet told me to come to this mountain and climb to the summit."

Hilt blinked, then his eyes narrowed in intensity. "The Prophet? Tell me, what did he look like?"

"Well, he was . . . his face . . ." Her brow wrinkled in confusion and she paused for a moment to search her memories, "I-I don't know how to describe him, just his presence. He just . . . he just felt right. Like I was safe with him and that he would never lead me wrong."

Hilt stared at her for a few seconds before placing his face in his hands, "Oh blast it all. How did he know I would be coming this way? Blast!"

"Excuse me?" she said, wide eyed at his reaction.

He put up a conciliatory hand. "Forgive my language. It's just that he always does this. He makes people a promise and shoves them in my path." The next time he saw the Prophet he would be sure to tell him about it too. Hilt shook his head and sighed. "I suppose my mission will have to be placed on hold."

Hilt reached for a leather strip that hung around his neck and pulled a slender tube made of a smooth gray wood out from under his chainmail vest. He lifted it to his lips and blew. There was no audible sound, but he felt it warm against his fingers and knew his message had been received. He nodded and tucked it back under his shirt.

"What are you doing?" she asked.

"I am telling my companion that I need his assistance." Hilt said. "He left Reneul before I did, but he has been taking his time. If I had not taken this detour I would have caught up to him by nightfall."

"But how-? Why . . .?" Her eyes widened in comprehension. "Wait. No-no. You're not coming with me."

"Oh, yes I am" Hilt said. He turned and strode parallel to the piles of rock that dotted the mountainside. "Come along. It would be best to stay out of the area the gorcs marked. They wouldn't warn their own people away without good reason."

"But-!" She hesitated, then hurried after him. "You didn't listen. I said 'You're *not* coming with me.'"

"And yet I am," Hilt replied. He paused and looked back at her. "You know, since we are to be taking this little journey together, I really should ask your name."

"Beth," she said. "But I still haven't agreed-."

He gave her a deep bow. "Beth, my lady, so nice to meet you. My name is Hilt. And don't worry, as soon as I get you to the top of this peak, I will take my leave and you will not have to see me again." He turned and continued along the slope, glad that the first winter snows had not come yet. The slope was steep and footing was hard enough as it was.

She followed behind him in silence for a while, which suited him just fine. The line of white stone markers eventually curved and turned up the steep slope of the mountainside and Hilt followed it, skirting the edge of the line they marked. The ground was a bit rocky and stubbled with tufts of grass for easy footing, but it was a strenuous hike nonetheless. Hilt fumed that the Prophet had stuck him with such an arduous task.

He kept looking back at the woman to make sure she was holding up. She trudged along right behind him with her skirts held up in bunched fists to keep from entangling herself. Her face was red and she was breathing quite heavily, but to her credit she wasn't complaining. Luckily there was no sign that the gorcs had followed them.

They hiked to the top of the incline. The ground leveled off and the path was flat for a while before the next rise, so Hilt stopped so she could rest. He sat on a large rock and watched her stumble over and plop down on another rock a few feet away. She slumped over and rested her forearms on her knees.

Hilt eyed her curiously. "So Beth, my lady, the Prophet tells you to climb a mountain, and you come wearing that?"

She gave him an irritated glance. "It's what I had on at the time."

"But where did you come from? There are no villages anywhere nearby and you aren't wearing a pack or anything. Do you have supplies? Food? Water?"

Her irritation turned into a glare. "He told me to go, and I went. What about you? You leave on an important mission from Reneul of all places going someplace urgently, and you throw it all away to climb a mountain with a woman that you obviously find quite crazy. All you have is that small pack on your back. Not exactly mountain climbing gear I would think."

"I am a named warrior. I can take care of myself," Hilt replied.

Beth snorted. "Pfft! Named warrior. Right!"

Hilt lifted his arm and showed her the rune on the back of his hand.

"Oh," she said. "I didn't-."

"It's usually the first thing people notice," he remarked.

"Well, it's not like I go around checking the back of people's hands all the time just to make sure they're not named."

"It covers the whole back of my hand. It's pretty hard to miss," Hilt pointed out. "Didn't you see me fighting?"

"I know a lot of good fighters and none of them are named," she said. Hilt rolled his eyes. "What? I'm supposed to see your fighting skill and say, 'oooh, he must be a named warrior'? Do I need to check your palms too just to make sure you're not a named wizard as well?"

"Don't be ridiculous." Hilt said. He shook his head and stood. "Let us start this over, shall we?" He cleared his throat. "Good morning, Madam. I am Sir Hilt, a named warrior come to take you down off this mountain before you get yourself killed."

He looked at her expectantly. She just stared back at him.

"Well," Hilt prompted. "Your turn. Come on."

A slight smile touched the corner of her mouth and she replied, "Why hello, Sir Hilt. I am Beth and I am climbing this mountain because the Prophet told me to. I might let you tag along if you ask nicely."

Hilt smiled. "Very good then. Since we are to be travel companions, would you mind if I take stock of our situation?"

She laid back on the rock and stretched out her legs. "Sure, go ahead."

"The good news is that as far as I can tell, the gorcs haven't followed us," he said.

"Good," she yawned.

"The problem is that it is going to take us maybe two days to climb to the top if we can make good time. We haven't had any snow yet, but it is going to get cold especially at night." He paused and looked at her again. "Is that dress really all you brought?"

"Do I look like I'm hiding anything?" she said, resting back on her elbows.

Hilt frowned. "How did you get here?" She just stuck out her feet in response so he tried again. "Perhaps the better question is where did you come from? There are no villages for miles from here."

"Pinewood," she said.

"You walked all the way here from Pinewood? You would have had to travel all the way through the Tinny Woods!" He was impressed with the woman's ability to survive. The place was crawling with moonrats and the foul creatures would eat anything alive or dead.

"I was in the woods when the Prophet found me. He told me to go and I went."

"But how did you survive?"

She sighed. "I don't know. I just walked east. When I was thirsty, there was a stream. When I was hungry, there were berries.

At night I dug under the leaves and slept. I never saw a single moonrat. I heard them of course, but never saw a single glowing eye. Since then I haven't worried. The Prophet said I could do it, so I know I can."

"So what did he tell you?" he asked.

"I told you," she said with a dull stare. "Climb the mountain."

"What were his instructions?" Hit prodded, growing tired of her obstinance. "What exactly did he say to you?"

"He said, 'Walk to the east. On the far side of the woods is a mountain. Climb to the top and you will find the answer you seek.' I said, 'When do I leave?' He said, 'Go now.' I said, 'Now? Wearing this?' He said, 'Yes.' I said, 'Shouldn't I prepare first? Pack supplies?' He said, 'If you go now, you will have everything you need.' I said, 'Okay.' Then I started walking."

Hilt looked at her askance. "You're fooling with me aren't you?"

Beth threw up her hands. "Fine. Believe me or not. That's what he said."

There was truth in her eyes and Hilt had to accept it. "Very well. It looks like the Prophet has provided our course. Nothing specific as usual, just, 'go up the mountain.' Let us see what means he has provided us with. What do you have on you, besides your dress? Anything?"

"And my underclothes, but no," she said. "Thick wool socks on my feet, my shoes, and a needle and spool of thread that I had forgotten were in my pocket when I left. I had a hairpin but I broke it trying to pick the lock on the treasure chest I found back in the forest."

"You what?" Hilt said, eyebrows raised.

"Now that time I was fooling with you," she said, stone faced.

Hilt blinked at her, then laughed. "You did throw me off, there."

She was unable to suppress a smile in return, "So the

named warrior laughs?"

"You don't know me. I am quick with a laugh," Hilt replied. "But still, a needle and thread are a commodity to take note of. As for me, I am carrying my swords, a waterskin, a dagger, a blanket, a coil of rope, my flame stick, some leather strips, some parchment, a quill and inkwell, some dried meat, and half a hard loaf of bread. It seems we shall have to find nourishment along the way."

"You carry all that in your little pack?" she asked, dubiously eyeing the bundle strapped behind his shoulders,.

"I am an efficient packer," he replied. Too much bulk or weight hampered his movements and he never knew when he might need to draw his swords for battle. "Now we should really keep moving. I would like to put a lot more distance between us and those gorcs by sundown."

She stood with a groan. "You worry about the gorcs? They didn't give you much trouble before."

Hilt snorted. "Gorcs are little trouble in the daylight. But at night, they could ambush us and with enough numbers I could have trouble protecting you. Come, let's continue."

He stood and resumed his route along the line of stone markers. They stretched along, small white dots in the mountainside as far as his eye could see, extending the length of the flat area and continuing up another steep slope. It was going to be a hard climb. Beth hurried up next to him, holding up her skirts as she kept pace. Her mouth was twisted like she wanted to say something, but they traversed the flat and rocky stretch of mountainside and nearly reached the next slope before she spoke.

"I still don't understand why you've decided to protect me," she said finally. "You said you were on a mission. Why the sudden change of heart? Why put the mission aside to help a woman past her prime on a hopeless quest?"

Hilt smiled. "My lady, you may not be a maiden, but you are hardly past your prime." She was probably near forty, but he gave a kind guess. "What are you, thirty?"

She wasn't fooled and gave him a knowing glare. "Thirty five."

Hilt shrugged. "Still younger than I, and I am most definitely not out of my prime, thank you."

"My age isn't the point," she said, letting go of her dress with one hand to waggle a finger at him. "You were all set to carry me down that mountain until I mentioned the Prophet. What made you change your mind?"

"I am a named warrior. This happens from time to time."

"What hap-!" As she stepped over a rock, her foot caught in the frayed hem of her dress. She tripped forward and fell to the ground, banging one knee and skinning the palms of her hands as she tried to catch herself.

Hilt stopped to help her up. He bent to grasp her arm, but reared back as she let out a stream of curses. He stood stunned and watched while she rose to her feet on her own and stomped her feet, cussing all the while, ending with, "I hate this dress!"

She turned and directed her glare at Hilt, who stood with hands raised, his face not betraying his thoughts. "What?" Beth spat. "I told you I'm a base born woman!"

"If I might make a suggestion, my lady." Hilt began.

"Do you want a black eye?" she said, shaking a quivering fist at him.

Hilt paused. "No. But If I may-."

"Stop calling me 'My lady'. I am not your lady. I am a regular person who is having a very bad year! My name is Beth. Call me Beth!"

"I am sorry," Hilt said. He saw tears in her eyes and realized that there was much more to her story than she had told him. "Beth, I have a suggestion. Something that might help with your current difficulty."

"Wings? Can you sprout wings and fly me up this mountain?" She asked, wide eyed. A moment of silence stretched between them and a chuckle escaped her lips. She burst out laughing. She sat down on the ground and laughed until tears streamed down her face. "Gah! This is all so ridiculous! I'm sorry. I am sorry, Sir Hilt. I am crazy and I am sorry. Sorry for yelling at you. Sorry for dragging you up here after me. Sorry for everything."

"It's okay. It's okay." Hilt crouched beside her and offered her a hand. A note of sternness entered his voice. "Beth. Stand up."

She accepted his hand and allowed him to pull her to her feet. While she dusted off her dress, he pulled his waterskin from its place at his side. He tossed it to her.

"Drink," he said and she did so gratefully. He took off his small pack and opened it up, pulling out several long strips of leather.

"Thank you," She said, wiping her mouth as she handed the waterskin back to him. He took it from her and replaced it at his side, then slung his pack back over his back.

"Now Beth, as I was trying to say, your dress is a nuisance. If you try to climb the mountain like this you are going to end up falling off a cliff or something. Now," He lifted the leather strips and drew his dagger. She eyed the dagger and took a step back. He held it out to her hilt first. "What I am suggesting, is that we turn that dress into bloomers."

"What?"

"Do you know what I am talking about? It may be more of a south-eastern style, but . . ."

"Oh! Of course!" Beth smiled and took the dagger and leather strips from him. She began cutting the skirts of her dress down the middle. "Oh, I wish I had thought of it before! Some times I am so stu-. Hey! Turn around."

"Sorry," Hilt said and turned his back to her as she continued her work, splitting the skirt and tying one half to each leg with the leather strips. When she had finished, she told him to turn back around.

"What do you think?" The leather strips looked like they were trying to contain a pair of ridiculously puffy trousers. She lifted one leg to show her freedom of movement.

"If I didn't know better, I would think you've done this before," Hilt replied, stifling a laugh.

She handed the dagger back to him. "It was a fabulous idea. I would do a cartwheel if not for my aching palms."

"Very good, shall we continue on?" Without waiting for a response he started up the slope, keeping an eye out for the path with the easiest footing.

He soon found a narrow trail worn into the mountainside that ran more or less parallel to the white stone markers. It seemed that the gorcs traversed this slope fairly often. This was fortunate, for it made the going easier, but it also meant that they could run into some of the creatures at any time. Hilt narrowed his senses, looking for signs of recent activity and listening for any sounds that could come from unwanted company. All he heard however was the scrape of their feet against the rocks and Beth humming a tune under her breath.

She was enjoying herself despite the steep climb. Being freed from the dress had put her in a good mood. Hilt was grateful for that, but at the same time, her humming was terribly out of tune. The worst part was that he recognized the song. It was one of his favorite tavern drinking songs and she was butchering it. She continued on, repeating the same verse over and over, each time just a little bit off. Finally he had had enough.

Hilt turned and said in what he hoped was a reasonable tone of voice, "No-no no. I believe you have that wrong. You see, the tune ends, '*and they all gave her a spaaankiiing.*'"

"What song did you think I was humming?" she asked.

"The Farmer's Drunken Daughter."

She laughed. "No. It was, The Dusty Dog's Last Laugh."

"No you weren't. That song goes, '*when the cobbler threw out the dry boooooones.*"

"Pff! Where did you learn the song?" She shook her head. "It goes, 'when the cobbler threw out the dryyyyyy bones!"

Her singing was even worse than her humming. Hilt grit his teeth. "I-. No-. Look that's not the point. It doesn't matter what the song is. Just-. Shh! New rule. No singing or humming."

"No humming?" she wrinkled her nose. "Why is that a rule?"

"Look, we are following a gorc trail. I am trying to listen for signs that they are close, so shh!"

She looked around at the barren rocky mountainside. "Where would they be hiding?"

"This is their land. Not ours. They know where to hide. Just-just be silent until I am sure," Hilt said.

"Fine," she said with a shrug and they continued on.

The trail was well used and free of debris. It meandered back and forth in a series of switchbacks that took them up the steepest part of the incline. They made good time, but as they neared the top, Hilt's concerns proved to be well founded. The sound of drums and gorc chanting began to echo down from the top of the ridge.

They crept up the last few switchbacks until they neared the top. Hilt motioned her to stay silent and left the trail, slowly climbing up the last stretch of the slope to peer over the top. Fifty feet ahead rose a sheer cliff thirty feet high. The trail they were on headed towards the cliff, then took a right and ran alongside it, leading to a wooded area bristling with pine trees. The sounds of the gorc camp came from that direction and he could see smoke wafting up from behind the trees. To his left, the line of white stone markers stretched on, ending at the cliff face. He swore under his breath.

Hilt slid back down to the trail and made sure to whisper to make sure his voice didn't carry to the gorcs. "I'm afraid we have three choices, none of them particularly good." He turned to see Beth lying on her side next to a large flat bounder, peering underneath. She reached one hand under the rock.

"Just a second, you sucker . . . there!" Beth rolled to her knees and stood, dragging out a long brown snake. She gave Hilt a triumphant smile and lifted it by the tail. It arched and hissed trying to reach her, but she kept it at arms length. "Got it!"

Hilt put a finger to his lips and raised a cautioning hand, then slowly drew one sword, and whispered, "Beth. Listen carefully. Drop it and back away. That is a Brown Viper. Very poisonous!"

She rolled her eyes and whispered back, "I'm not going to let it bite me!"

"Just put it down," Hilt said, ready to lop off its head as soon as she let go.

"Oh for goodness sake," Beth said and in one fluid motion, swung the snake up over her head in a wide arc and whipped it against the rock. Then as it lay stunned and motionless, she took one step and crushed its head with the heel of her boot. She smiled at him sweetly. "And that, Sir Hilt is how a Pinewood lady hunts for supper."

"I . . ." Hilt didn't know how to react. He was both confused and impressed by this woman in equal measure. He sheathed his sword. "Very good then. Viper dead. So . . ."

She folded her arms. "Three bad choices?"

"Yes, three choices. At the top of the incline, we can either follow the trail to the right towards a gorc encampment, we can go straight and climb a sheer cliff, or we can go left and cross over the line of white markers."

She frowned. "Why are we so afraid of crossing those white rock piles again?"

Hilt closed his eyes, then took a deep breath and released it slowly. "It could be anything. Creatures, natural hazards . . . For the gorcs to mark a part of their own territory in this way means that they fear what ever is over that line."

"Ah, but I've got you with me, right? Nothing you can't handle." She smacked him on the shoulder, looped the dead snake over her arm and headed up the incline.

Hilt again considered knocking her unconscious and dragging her back down the mountain. Instead he joined her at the top, made sure that there were no gorcs in sight and led her to the left, crossing the white markers.

II

The land beyond the white markers sloped upward as Hilt had hoped and they were able to hike to a high spot where the cliff face was only eight feet instead of the thirty he had seen when they left the trail. He was able to scale it easily and help Beth up behind him.

It became obvious to Hilt as they turned up the mountainside, why the gorcs stayed out of the area. The slope was gradual and rocky, but interspersed among the rocks rose plumes of steam.

"Ugh, what's that smell?" Beth complained with a grimace.

"Sulfur," said Hilt. "Among other things. Evidently this mountain is a bubbler."

"Bubbler?"

"Yes, well that's what my commander called it back in my guard days. It's a place where the earth beneath the mountain is so hot that it pushes chemicals and gasses to the surface. This place is one step away from becoming a volcano." He held out his hand. "Come, stay by my side. The way ahead will be treacherous."

She hesitated. "You want me to hold your hand?"

"It would be the safer course, yes. That way if the ground crumbles beneath you, I can pull you to safety."

She eyed the offered hand dubiously, "And what if it crumbles beneath you? You going to pull me in with you?"

Hilt threw up his hands in surrender. "Fine, Beth. If you don't trust my intentions, just stay close. I have been in these types of areas before and know what to look for." He turned and began walking towards the rising plumes of steam.

Her face reddened a bit and she opened her mouth as if to say something, but she just followed behind him instead. To his surprise, she stayed close as he had requested.

The air grew warmer as they approached the active area. Clusters of trees appeared here and there growing from small earthy areas between stretches of rock. Hilt began to feel a low steady vibration beneath his feet.

A dull roar echoed down the mountainside as they drew nearer to the steam. Beth's hand latched onto his.

"What is this?" he asked, stopping in surprise.

"I do trust you," she said. Her voice was steady, but her fingers were trembling. "I know I just met you this morning, but you have been nothing but a gentleman and . . . I'm sorry about before."

Hilt saw a hint of fear in her blue eyes and wondered if it was the area they were approaching or the fact that she was holding his hand that frightened her. He smiled and gave her hand a reassuring squeeze.

"There is no need to apologize. Your reaction was understandable. Not all men are trustworthy," he said. She nodded and gave him a weak smile in return. He added, "Though the area ahead is dangerous, it will also be fascinating. You will see."

They continued forward, hand in hand, Hilt making sure to stay on solid slabs of rock as much as possible. They passed bubbling mud pots, hissing steam vents, and rivulets of warm water filled with multicolored algae. Beth soon forgot her fears and ooed and ahhed at each wonder. Hilt had to make sure to keep her from getting too close.

They rounded one particularly large boulder and came upon a wide steaming pool of water. The surface was calm and the water was clear and blue. Hilt estimated it to be several meters deep in the center. It looked inviting.

"It's beautiful," Beth said, gazing at the steaming pool with longing eyes. "Ohh, it would be so nice to bathe in warm water again."

"Not a good idea," Hilt warned. He pointed to the far edge of the pool where a frog floated, belly up. "When I was campaigning on academy assignment, one of our men fell into a hot pool like that. He boiled alive before we could fish him out."

"Oh," she said with a disappointed pout. "W-well if it's that hot at least the water is clean, right? Maybe we could gather some?"

"I wouldn't suggest drinking it," he said. "In active areas like this, it might not be just water. There could be acid or any number of other toxic things in there. Another man on that journey drank from a hot stream and died vomiting blood. His name was Henry. Henry the Bold."

"Oh. How horrible," she said.

"Nah, don't feel sorry for him. Henry was a good soldier, but he was a horrible man," Hilt said. "He liked killing a little too much."

"Oh . . . good riddance then, I guess." She shrugged. "Well! I'm tired. Can we rest? Are you hungry? I'm starving."

"Uh, yes. Sure," Hilt said. It was late in the afternoon and they hadn't eaten. "I suppose we can stop and eat. But I really don't want to tarry long. I would like to be away from this area before we stop for the night."

"Oh." She looked disappointed. "I suppose that means we don't have time to build a fire. I was kind of looking forward to cooking this snake. I'm getting tired of carrying it around, actually."

Hilt chuckled. "To tell you the truth, I've been dreading having to eat it."

"You don't like snake?"

"Beth, my lady, I don't fancy myself a picky man. I have been on many long campaigns and I have been forced to eat many things over the years. There are only a few of them I've hoped to forget, and almost all of those were reptilian in nature."

Beth grinned. "That, Sir Hilt, is because you have never

eaten snake prepared by someone who knows how to cook it."

"Ah. Very well, but for now, why don't we just eat some of the bread and dried meat I brought with me. Maybe tonight, if it's safe, we can build a fire and cook that snake for you."

Beth sighed. "Okay."

Hilt took the food out of his pack and divided it between them. The meat was well salted and it was tough, but flavorful. The bread was hard and barely edible, but they were hungry enough that it didn't matter. After they each drank from the waterskin, Hilt noted that there wasn't much left. They would need to find some water soon.

"You didn't answer my question," Beth said around a mouthful of the hard bread.

"Didn't I?" Hilt asked, not sure what she was talking about. "What question was that?"

"Back down there just before I fell on my face. I asked you why you were helping me. You never answered." She stared at him expectantly.

Hilt gave her a shrug. "It was my duty."

"Why?" she asked, "What does being a named warrior have to do with my quest?"

"It's a matter of pride." Hilt looked down for a moment and when he looked back at her, he wore a weary smile. "It's a long tale."

"Most tales are," she said.

"Very well, but for you to truly understand, I must start at the beginning." Hilt gathered his thoughts for a moment, staring into the depths of the steaming pool. "I was born George Slarr, son of Duke Andres Slarr of Gladstone. As the first born son of the Duke, it would one day be my responsibility to take over stewardship of Gladstone, but I didn't want to rule. I saw what the responsibilities of being a Duke did to my father and I hated it. When I was young, I met several named warriors that came to visit my father. I idolized those men. I wanted more than anything to be as good as them. A named warrior has the highest respect among fighters and more than that, a named warrior is free. Free to do as he wished, no longer tied to land or country.

"Oh how I wanted that. I wanted to shed my father's name and be my own man. I trained hard. I trained with my father's soldiers, I trained in foreign lands. When I was nineteen I went to the Battle Academy and it was there that I gained the first step towards my independence. I earned a man's name. They called me George the Wind. I loved that name. The wind. That's how I felt during battle, dancing through my enemies like a force of nature. I was brash, arrogant, cocksure. Back then I was sure I was invincible."

Beth's eyebrow rose. "And that has changed?"

Hilt paused. "Do you want me to finish this story?"

She raised a hand. "Please go on. Please do. It is a fascinating story. I am enthralled, truly. I just wonder how this answers my question."

"I am getting to that, just . . ." Hilt frowned. "Do you know how many people I have told this story to?"

She wisely didn't respond.

Hilt waited for a moment, gauging her response, then cleared his throat and continued, "But even as George the Wind, I was still a Slarr. My father expected me to come home as soon as my academy contract was over and marry some noble girl he had picked out for me. After I graduated, I spent my contracted time campaigning in the wilds, fighting monsters and honing the skills I had learned. Two years later my contract was up, as was my time of freedom. It was time to go home. It was time to face my duty."

"You could have run," she said.

"That's what my friends said. But it was never really an option. That would have crushed my father and dishonored my family. I couldn't do that. My only way out was the Bowl of Souls."

"You alluded to that before. But how does that help?" Beth asked. "How would being named save you from your family responsibilities?"

"Ah, well a named warrior cannot hold a noble rank. It is in the country bylaws and it is part of the history of the Bowl of Souls. By being named, I would be required to forfeit my birthright and yet still bring my family great honor. My younger brother would carry on the Slarr name. It was what he wanted anyway. He wasn't as highly favored by our father and that had always rankled him. It was the perfect answer and it was the chance I had been training for. I had these two swords made and then I went to the Mage School to stand before the bowl."

"I can't imagine what it must have been like. Leaving your life to chance like that." Beth said. "Walking up to the bowl must have been terrifying."

Hilt smiled. "Yes, it's true that very few are chosen. It's also true that a warrior only gets one chance to be named. Once refused, he cannot come back again. I knew that going in. And if that had happened I was prepared to go back and do my duty. However, I was confident. I knew I was as good as I was ever going to be. The day that I stood before the Bowl of Souls, I knew that I had worked hard and I was ready. I was ready for the freedom, and to tell you the truth, I was ready for the praise. I was ready for the acclaim."

He gripped the hilts of his swords and as he continued he was unable to keep the pride out of his voice. "When I dipped my blades in the water of the bowl, it accepted me and the name that shot from my lips was Hilt. I had reached it. The pinnacle. My dream."

"Wait, *you* said it?" she asked, her brow wrinkled in confusion. "You named yourself?"

"No. The bowl named me. But that's how it works. It doesn't have a mouth to speak with, so it speaks through the person being named." From the expression on her face, Hilt knew she didn't understand. He looked up as he struggled to put the experience into words. "I'll try to explain better. It . . . the Bowl of Souls reaches inside you and just . . . you can feel the vastness of it just searching the core of you and this-this pressure builds and you get the sense in your mind of something huge and important happening. Then without even knowing it, you start chanting some strange language and the name grows in your mind until it is too big to contain and it springs from your throat with a great shout. Then you're standing there and the rune has appeared on your hand and on your weapon and it-it-. It's wonderful."

He looked back at Beth to find her staring open-mouthed. He chuckled. Pleased at her reaction. "But there is one thing no one tells you about being named. You aren't really free."

She rose a shaking hand and pointed over his shoulder. "L-look."

Hilt felt the familiar chill of danger and drew his swords in one swift motion as he spun around. Standing behind him just a few yards away swaying and blinking stupidly were three trolls. All at once, they lifted their long arms tipped in vicious claws and screeched.

His well-trained mind assessed the situation. They were mountain trolls, seven feet tall and gangly, with beady eyes and cavernous mouths full of rows of teeth. A thick layer of slime dripped from their grey skin.

Trolls were mindless creatures driven only by hunger and they were hard to kill, regenerating from any wound. The only way to kill them for sure was to light them on fire. The slime that coated their skin was highly flammable and they went up quicker than lamp oil. Unfortunately, Hilt didn't have a fire source handy.

Hilt erupted into motion, spinning and slicing. The most important thing when fighting multiple trolls was to disable them right away. His first cuts went at the outstretched arms of the closest troll, lopping off its hands at the wrists. He ducked the swipe of the second troll and swung low, severing one of its legs at the knee.

As it crashed to the ground, the first troll tried to pull him in with the stumps of its arms, its open mouth descending on him. He met its mouth with the tip of one sword, piercing its soft upper pallet and continued through its brain to stick out the top of its skull. He twisted the blade and shoved its quivering hulk atop the other downed beast, and left his sword stuck in its skull while he turned to face the third.

It was charging toward Beth, who was backing away but not fast enough. He wouldn't be able to reach her side before it struck. Trolls were filthy creatures and even a scratch from their claws could cause a serious infection.

Hilt gripped his remaining sword with both hands and called out to the magic in the blade. The sword was ready and eager. The magic gathered quickly. He stepped forward, spun, and released it with a mighty two-handed swing. A gust of wind hurtled from the blade and caught the troll mid-stride, sending it sprawling into the steaming blue pool. Beth stumbled and fell on her rump in surprise, but she seemed otherwise unharmed. Hilt turned back to the other two trolls.

The troll with the sword stuck in its skull still lay quivering, but Hilt had to jump out of the way to avoid the claws of the second troll, which launched itself at him with its one good leg. It gathered itself and leapt towards him again. He jumped back out of the reach of its attack and swung his blade. He called up the magic of the blade again, but this time narrowed the power of the wind down to a fine razor edge.

Though the tip of his blade missed its face by inches, the power of the magic took off its head from the nose up. The troll crashed to the ground and the top of its skull rolled several feet away and rattled to a stop.

Hilt stabbed the sword into its back and hurriedly took off his small pack.

"Beth!" he barked. She looked at him from the place where she sat, stunned. "You all right?"

"I-I. I never . . " She stared at him, eyes wide, her face blank. He had seen that expression many times before in the eyes of men after battle. He needed to snap her out of it quick, and the best way to do that was to give her something to do.

"Beth, come here! Hurry, I need your help."

She shook her head and blinked away her stupor before climbing to her feet. "W-what?"

"Here, help me drag their bodies together. It's only a few moments before they start moving again," he said. He grabbed one of the troll's arms. "Careful, they're slippery."

"But their heads . . ." she said eyeing the top of the trolls head which sat just a few feet away. The eyes were twitching.

"They really don't use their brains much and they regenerate fast. It's surprising how quickly they recover. That's why I left my other sword in the first one's head." He gave what he hoped was a reassuring smile. "Come on, grab its leg. Just don't let your hands slip. Their claws are sharp. You don't want to cut yourself."

She lifted its one remaining foot. "Um, gross," she said, grimacing at the feeling of its slime covered skin. She wrapped both hands around its ankle and helped Hilt pull it over and toss it down on top of the body of the other troll.

"Where is the other one?" His eyes were on the deep blue pool. The surface was still once more.

"Um, I don't think it ever came out," she said.

He walked over quickly and looked into the water. The troll had sunk to the bottom of the pool and stayed motionless, its claws reaching upward, its mouth hanging open in a silent screech of rage.

"Huh. What do you know? It drowned. I never drowned a troll before," Hilt said.

"W-will it stay dead?" Beth asked.

"I imagine so. That liquid is so hot that it probably cooked it. A cooked troll is a dead troll." He turned back to her. "Speaking of . . ."

He tossed something to her, which she caught clumsily. It was a wooden dowel about the length of her thumb and there was a leather cap covering one end. "What is it?"

"It's my flame stick. Got it as a gift from a wizard friend years ago," Hilt replied. He walked over and retrieved his swords, wrenching them free from the troll's bodies. "Take the cap off the end, but be careful not to lose it. It's made of firedrake leather.

Hard stuff to get ahold of."

She pulled the cap off and saw a round metal button imbedded in the end of the stick. There was a symbol carved into the metal. "That's a fire rune."

Hilt nodded. "Exactly." He extended one sword out to her blade first. It was dripping with troll slime. "Rub the metal on the tip of the sword. Carefully, now."

When she brushed the flame stick against the sword, there was a tiny spark. The troll slime combusted and the entire length of the blade was set ablaze. Hilt touched the sword to the bodies of the trolls and with a whoosh, they went up in flame. He walked over to the body parts that he had lopped off of the trolls and speared them quivering on the end of his sword before flicking them into the fire.

"Would you put the cap back on? Just be careful not to touch the metal." Beth put the leather cap back over the end and stared at the burning trolls transfixed until Hilt came to her side. He looked at her with worried eyes. "Are you okay, Beth?"

She swallowed and handed him the fire stick. "I don't know."

He tucked it into his pocket and grabbed her hand. "Come. Let's continue on. You'll feel better as we get away from here."

Hilt hoped he was right. She seemed quite shaken up. He was relieved when only a few yards later, she shot him a glare and said, "I've seen battles before, you know."

"I'm sure you have," he said.

"Not trolls, but I've lived in Pinewood for fifteen years. I've seen goblins, gorcs, orcs, bears, moonrats . . . I even watched the town guard kill a giant once," she said. "So don't go treating me like some moon-eyed girl that can't handle a little violence!"

"I wouldn't dream of it," he said in all sincerity. She set her jaw and narrowed her eyes at him suspiciously, but let him continue leading her along by the hand.

Hot pots and steam vents bubbled and hissed all around them. They had to backtrack a few times to avoid some particularly dangerous footing, but a half hour later they had passed the most active area and the air began to smell fresh again. Still, she didn't let go of his hand.

"What was that you did back there?" she asked. "When you knocked that troll into the pool, I mean."

"That was my sword," he said. "Northwind, I call her. She hangs on my right hip. Southwind is the other. He hangs on my left."

"Magic swords . . ." she said. "I've heard of them before, but that was pretty impressive."

"Thank you," he said with a smile. "When I was ready to go to the Bowl of Souls, I knew that I needed a special set of swords. I found a master smith that knew how to work runes into the metal and I commissioned them. He, uh . . . took my name to heart when he forged them."

"George the Wind," she said. "I saw the air runes on the hilts, but I thought they were just for show."

"You seem to know a lot about runes," he said and she just shrugged in response. There was so much about this woman he didn't know. "Well, you're right. When he handed them to me, he told me he had made me some 'little breezes'."

They walked several minutes in silence before she spoke again.

"I-I'm sorry about before, Hilt. I don't usually act like this. It's just that I have hunted animals all my life and for some reason when I'm around, the creatures are calm as a kitten. They never attack me. Not snakes, moonrats, bears, anything. But when that troll came at me, the look of hunger in its eyes . . . I've never felt so helpless before. He was going to eat me, tear me limb from limb and I-I had no way to stop him."

"Bah! Not true," Hilt said and gave her his most disarming smile. "You had me."

Her mouth twitched and she looked as though she didn't know whether to laugh or smack him. Finally she returned his smile. "I'm glad you came with me, Sir Hilt. I want you to know . .

."

"What do you want me to kno-?" She placed a finger against his lips, stopping him mid-word. Her eyes were wide with fear as she pulled the finger away and pointed up the slope to the right.

Hilt cursed his luck. Just over the next ridge, walking down the slope towards them were four trolls. Two of them were standard mountain trolls like the ones he had dealt with earlier, but the other two were different, bent and misshapen. That was not a good sign.

"Alright. We'll be okay, We'll just have to go up the other side of the slope." She was still staring at the swaying trolls as they approached. He reached up and gently turned her face towards his. He waited until her eyes latched onto his. "Listen to me, Beth. Trolls can't see well. At this distance, they can't make us out. Their main senses are smell and taste and we are downwind from them right now."

She swallowed and nodded.

He grabbed one of the leather cords around his neck and pulled a pouch out from under his shirt. He opened it up and dumped its contents, mainly gold and silver coins, into his hand and shoved them into his pocket. He then took the fire stick out and tucked it into the pouch.

"I want you to hold onto this for me, okay?" He wrapped her fingers around the pouch and hung the cord over her neck. "Fire is the best weapon against trolls. If we have to face them again, you light a stick or something, anything you can find. You'll be ready for them."

The leather creaked as she tightened her grip on the pouch. "You bet I will."

They trotted to the left, putting some distance between them and the approaching trolls, then turned and began climbing again. As they navigated the rock strewn slope, Hilt kept a sharp eye on the monsters' progress. So far, the trolls had continued on their path, seemingly oblivious to their presence.

As they were rounding one particularly large boulder, Hilt's foot slipped. He caught himself, but swore as he looked down. "Blast! Troll sign."

"What's that?" Beth asked.

"Trolls leave slime trails wherever they go like-like . . . great lines of snot." He scraped his boot off on a nearby rock. "This one was fresh."

"It looks like a snail trail." Her nose wrinkled and she pointed to the path ahead. "Look!"

Long glistening lines crisscrossed the path ahead. Hilt looked back to the trolls on the other side of the slope. The beasts had stopped and stood swaying slightly, long tongues hanging out as they tasted the air.

"Can we get around them if we climb up a bit more and cross back over?" she asked.

"No. The wind is blowing against us. If we climb past them, our scent will blow right to them. We have no choice but to keep going up this side."

As they picked their way up the slope, Hilt became sure that another battle was inevitable. There were troll trails everywhere, some dried and flaking away, others still wet. He had been wrong about the reason the gorcs had marked this area off. It wasn't the volcanic activity. This mountain had a troll infestation.

"How could there be so many trolls?" Beth asked.

"There must have been a battle," Hilt said. "Maybe the gorcs tried to fight the trolls and cut some of them to pieces. If you don't burn the bodies, they always grow back, one for every piece. Two of those trolls on the other side of the slope are misshapen. That only happens when a single troll is cut into too many pieces. Sometimes they don't grow back right."

"But what do they eat? Other than this snake, I haven't seen any wildlife around here," she said.

"That's a good point. Other than fire, starvation's the only thing that kills a troll. Maybe this infestation is recent. That would explain the missing wildlife."

The earth rumbled under their feet and an earsplitting chorus of screeches echoed across the slope in one long roar.

Beth wrapped her arms around him, her mouth open in silent terror and Hilt looked for the source of the sound. His eyes darted towards the trolls on the far side of the slope, but there was no way they had done it. To his surprise the trolls were running further down the mountainside away from the sound. As he watched, one of them lurched and fell, tumbling down in a shower of rocks. Hilt looked back to the top of the slope directly in from of them. The sound must have come from up there.

"Beth, my lady, those other trolls are gone. I think we can move to the other side now."

She looked up at him and back down to the fleeing trolls and nodded. She let go of him, her face red with embarrassment. "Sorry."

He grabbed her hand, but as they began to make their way back across the slope, screeches rang out from the top of the ridge. Two trolls ran down the slope towards them, arms outstretched, slaver dripping from their toothy maws.

Hilt stepped in front of Beth and drew his swords, willing the magic in the blades to form. He would have to cut them down quickly.

He started towards them, but to his surprise, they burst into flame, first one, then the other. Their screeches turned into screams and they ran off in opposite directions, before tripping and tumbling down the slope, setting trollsign trails ablaze as they went.

Hilt looked up to the top of the ridge and was surprised to see a small person walking down the slope towards them. He carried a gray wooden bow in one hand and a quiver and small pack were thrown across one shoulder. He had close cropped stubbly hair and pointed ears and his skin was dark and leathery. He looked ancient, the skin of his face so lined and wrinkled that Hilt could barely see his wise eyes staring out from under them. He walked down the rock strewn slope barefoot, wearing nothing but a loincloth.

"Yntri!" Hilt said in surprise, a wide grin on his face.

III

"So glad to see you. How did you get up here ahead of us?"

Yntri Yni was looking at Beth. He pointed at her and let out an accusatory series of clicks and whistles.

Beth gripped his arm. "Hilt. . . Who is that and why is he naked?"

"Uh, Beth, this is Yntri Yni. One of the ancient ones, weapon master of the Roo-Tan, and guardian of the Jharro Grove. He is my companion on my current mission. He is holy and deserving of the utmost respect." Then as an aside, he added, "And even I don't know why he chooses to dress like this. He doesn't feel the cold like you or I and . . . I'm just glad he covers the important parts."

Yntri shook a fist at him and clicked and whistled a series of demands.

"What is he upset about?" Beth asked.

"He is mad that I abandoned our mission for this detour," he explained. "Yntri, this is Beth. She is on a quest to climb to the peak of this mountain and I have agreed to escort her there."

The weathered old elf gave Hilt a dumbfounded expression and stomped his foot, berating him and letting out a string of curses in his ancient language.

"It's not like that, Yntri. I-." He swallowed. "Uh, Beth would you please tell Yntri Yni why I am helping you."

"I'm not sure that I know. You told me your whole life story earlier, but you still never got around to it," she reminded.

"Just-just tell him why you are climbing this mountain . . . please." Hilt said.

"So he understands the common tongue?" she asked. The elf was giving both of them a mean glare.

"Yes. He just doesn't speak it. He says his mouth's not made for it." He placed both hands together in a pleading gesture. "Just please tell him before he shoots me."

She nodded and smiled at the elf, then said out of the side of her mouth, "His name's In Tree a Knee, right?"

"Yntri Yni. Close, though," Hilt said.

She gave the ancient elf an awkward curtsey and said, "Mister Yntri Anee, I am Beth from Pinewood. I am climbing this mountain because the Prophet came to me and told me to. Sir Hilt for some reason has decided to accompany me and protect me until I reach the peak. I am sorry that this delays your mission. I don't mean to be a nuisance. Really, I don't."

At the mention of the Prophet, Yntri clapped one wrinkled hand over his face and shook his head, grumbling. At last he sighed and walked over to Beth, looking her up and down. She was just a few inches taller than him. He slung his bow over his shoulder and reached out and poked her, once in each shoulder, once in the stomach, and continued, working his way around her grabbing her arm, feeling various muscles.

"Ow! Hey! What's he doing?" she demanded.

"He is sizing you up." Hilt explained. "Evaluating your talent. It is a tradition among his people and an honor, really. Just bear with it."

"Okay but, I don't like being touched like thi-! Does he have to cup my butt?" Her face grew red as the elf ran his hand up her side and across her chest to rest over her heart. He paused for a moment, then leaned in and placed his ear between her breasts, listening to her heartbeat. Her jaw dropped in indignation and she glared at Hilt. "This had better stop now before I strangle him."

"Uh, she means it, Yntri," Hilt warned.

Yntri released her and took a step back. He smiled and

bowed to her, then spoke to Hilt.

Hilt's eyebrows raised in surprise. "He says that you are a strong woman and that he is very impressed. He says that you have a heart that is made for the bow. He says that it is a rare gift and that he is pleased because you are the second person he has met this year with such raw talent."

Yntri smiled and nodded and smacked her rump in agreement.

"Oh! You . . ." Her face twitched as she digested what he said. Hilt wondered if she would thank the elf or follow through on her promise to strangle him. Finally she took a deep breath, let it out, and said, "Thank you, Yntri. It's been several years since I shot a bow, though. And . . . since I know you can understand me, understand that if you smack my butt again, I will slap your face no matter how ancient you are."

The elf chuckled and nodded his head, clicking and whistling again.

"He says he likes you. He will accompany us and make sure you arrive to the top safely." Hilt did not add the part where Yntri told him that she had a fine figure and would make a great wife. The elf was constantly asking him why he wasn't married.

"Well, thank you again," Beth said, then her brow furrowed. "But how did you beat us here?"

Yntri clicked away and Hilt nodded, then told Beth, "He was on the far side of the mountain, when he received my signal. His bow told him we were ascending the slope so he came up from the other side."

"His bow told him?"

"His bow is made from the wood of the Jharro tree. The Jharro weapon forges a link with its master that is quite remarkably similar to the link that a named warrior has with his weapon. It's quite fascinating and one of the reasons why I went to live with his people in the first place. Anyway, the whistle he gave me is a piece of his bow and because I had it with me, he was able to track us down."

Yntri clicked at Hilt and stuck out his hand expectantly, Hilt nodded and lifted the small gray wooden whistle from around his neck and handed it to the elf. Yntri touched the whistle to his bow. It stuck to the wood and slowly began dissolving into it.

They were interrupted by a repeat of the horrible sound from earlier. The screeching roar echoed across the slope and Hilt saw a cloud of dust rise from just over the ridge. Beth gasped, clutching her hands over her ears and Hilt squeezed her shoulder with calm reassurance.

"Yntri, you came from over there. Did you see what made that sound?" The elf didn't answer. Hilt prodded, "That sounded like a hundred trolls back there. Are there so many?"

Yntri Yni set his jaw and stared back at him in silence.

Hilt felt a chill run up his spine. There was something the elf didn't want him to see. Whatever it was, it was a challenge. Yntri knew how he felt about challenges. "What is it, Yntri? How many are there?"

The elf held up one finger.

"You mean it?" Hilt laughed. He started towards the sound, but Yntri placed one hand on his chest, stopping him. The elf slowly shook his head, his eyes deadly serious. "What? I just want to see it. I have to see it."

"What are you talking about, Hilt?" Beth asked.

"I'm pretty sure it's a troll behemoth. I mean, it has to be." His heart was beating madly in his chest.

Beth's eyes darted from Hilt to Yntri and back. "What's that?"

"A troll behemoth is one of the ten monsters of legend; a troll with a rare disease. For some reason its healing ability goes berserk and it starts growing extra limbs, heads, eyes, claws, you name it, and as long as it keeps eating, it keeps growing." Hilt licked his lips and gripped his sword hilts to stop his fingers from twitching. "They are extremely rare and they are nearly impossible to kill. Only a few men are known to have done it."

Hilt had seen the bones of one once. A professor at the

Mage School had found the remains of one that had died of starvation. He had painstakingly reassembled it and had it on display in the back of the library. It had been enormous. Hilt saw it the day he was named and ever since he had ached to fight one.

Evidently Beth saw the worry in Yntri's face because she clutched Hilt's arm. "Lets go around to the other side. I don't want to see this thing."

"Don't worry. Just stay here with Yntri. I have to go look. I can't be this close to a legend and not go see it." He gave her a confident smile. "Don't worry. I got where I am by knowing my abilities. I'm not going to fight something I can't defeat. I'll be right back. I promise."

He gently pried her fingers from his arm and hiked toward the top of the ridge. There was a slight rumble at his feet as the behemoth roared again. Hilt grinned, and sweat broke out on his forehead. He would keep his promise. He wasn't about to fight a hopeless battle. He hadn't prepared for such a task after all. He would want torches and spears, barrels of oil, perhaps some fire arrows . . . but what if? What if it could be done?

Beth watched Hilt ascend the slope with a sinking feeling in her chest. She looked to the ancient elf. "He's going to try and fight it isn't he?"

Yntri Yni's dark look was the answer she hadn't wanted to see.

Hilt neared the top of the ridge and glanced back to see Beth and Yntri staring up at him. They were still standing where he had left them, which was good. If there truly was a troll behemoth nearby, he didn't want Beth seeing it.

Her reaction to the earlier troll attack had taken Hilt by surprise. Why had she been so shaken by it when before she had been so fearless? Her explanation of why the trolls had affected her didn't make sense. He had no reason to doubt her story, but the idea that she had gone through life near the Tinny Woods without ever being attacked by a creature was something he found difficult to fathom. Was it just odd luck or was there something else about her?

Hilt reached the top of the ridge and his nose wrinkled with the rancid smell of troll that hung in the air. He saw what Yntri Yni had already seen. The ground leveled out, then dipped slightly before rising into another rocky slope. He now had a pretty good idea where the behemoth was. Nearly every inch of ground was covered in slime trails, most of it leading from a wide cave mouth that yawned from the base of the slope ahead.

Hilt drew his swords and stepped forward cautiously, ready for an attack to come at any time. For that much slime to be around there must be dozens of trolls in the area. But he didn't see any. Where were they?

He hesitated in front of the entrance. What was he doing? Yes, the chance to see a legendary beast was hard to resist, but was it okay to leave Beth alone with Yntri when so many trolls were about? Yntri would be able to protect her just fine. He had lived for thousands of years near the troll swamps after all, and his fire arrows were quite effective. But Beth did not understand the ancient elf language and her willfulness could get them both in trouble.

Hilt's excitement was too great to be held back by doubts however, and he shook off his apprehension. He would be gone minutes at the most. He was just going to have a look at the beast.

Troll slime oozed from the cave mouth like an open sore. The behemoth had to be enormous. He wondered how far into the cave he would have to go to find it. The next question was how was he going to see? The light from outside would only illuminate so far into the interior and it would be foolhardy to attempt lighting a torch. One drip of flame in this slime and he would immolate himself.

Hilt peered inside. The ceiling was high enough that he could enter without bending over. Slime squelched around his feet as he eased into the cave and he was grateful that the boots he had chosen for the journey were calf high. A bright beam of light shown in from outside, illuminating everything in its path, but at the same time making it hard to see what was outside the beam.

Hilt stepped into the darkness and put the light at his back, waiting for his eyes to adjust. He listened carefully and heard bubbling along with a steady low throbbing sound. Splashes echoed out nearby. Something was coming towards him, something low to the ground. By then he could see just well enough to make out that it was a troll.

It was half a troll really. Just a torso with arms and a head, yet it dragged itself through the slime towards him, its beady eyes gleaming hungrily from the sunlight at Hilt's back. Hilt extended his right sword and watched its approach, wondering what had happened to the rest of its body. He reached into his bond with the sword and stepped towards the troll. He focused the air magic into an extension of his blade, and swung down.

The precise cut cleaved the troll's head in two and the air magic continued the cut down to its shoulder blades. The troll jittered on the floor silently and Hilt examined the stump of its lower half. The wound was ragged and torn, entrails still pouring out of it. Whatever had cut the thing in two had done so very recently. Hilt crept past it, knowing that it would heal quickly. He would have to finish his exploration fast or deal with it again on his way out.

At the back of the cave was a narrow opening and Hilt could see that this was the source of the slime that filled the cave. The flammable substance poured into the cave from this passage in a steady stream. Hilt edged up to the opening and peered inside. There was a faint glow coming from a chamber further down the passage along with a hot and humid stench. He hunched over and walked through the passageway, swords at the ready. The slime flow made for treacherous footing and he had to step carefully to keep from slipping.

The chamber beyond was enormous, easily three times the size of the cave entrance. Phosphorescent fungus lined the walls and ceiling, lending the area an eerie green light. The horrid smell and humidity were intense. In the center of the chamber, a wide pool bubbled and Hilt could see that underneath the slime was a boiling hot spring.

Passageways of multiple sizes and shapes opened up here

and there all along the chamber walls. Hilt saw the tiny reflections of a rat's eyes in the edge of one of these passageways. It was eating some of the glowing fungus and after watching it for a few moments Hilt understood how the behemoth survived in this place. The heat and moisture created the perfect environment to grow the fungus. The fungus was a food source for other vermin, and the behemoth ate the vermin.

Hilt's eyes widened as he looked to the rear of the chamber. In the darkest corner was a large pile of troll bodies. Hilt had seen nothing like it before. They lay motionless as if paralyzed. It looked as if someone had discarded hundreds of troll corpses in the corner, stacking them haphazardly. He stepped out of the passageway and moved closer to get a better look. Then the entire rear of the chamber shifted and Hilt realized that he had been mistaken. That was the behemoth.

It was a pulsating mass of glistening flesh. All along the surface of the behemoth, pieces of trolls were sticking out. No, that wasn't quite true. They were growing out of it. Heads, legs, arms, torsos, all protruding from it at different angles. Now he understood where the troll torso in the cave entrance had come from. It had been protruding from the behemoth and was scraped off on the cavern wall. The beast was so large it had to happen from time to time, and it explained why there were so many trolls in the area. If a piece of the behemoth broke free, it would eventually grow into a regular troll.

There was a shudder under his feet and the pool in the center of the room began to boil madly. Every head on the behemoth's body opened up into a wailing screech. A rush of air knocked Hilt off balance and he nearly slipped and fell. That was the sound they had heard earlier, the behemoth's roar. Luckily it hadn't been focused at him or it may have burst his eardrums.

Hilt realized he was looking at the behemoth's back. Its limbs and head had been shoved down passageways into other chambers, most likely in search of food. His fingers twitched with excitement and he felt the magic stirring within his swords. This was a good time to strike. Now, while its back was turned.

A voice echoed from the darkness behind him. "Hilt! You come out of there!"

Hilt winced. It was Beth. Why hadn't she obeyed his instructions?

The glistening bulk responded to the sound. It shivered and moved, sliding further into the chamber. Hilt could hear bones within the behemoth cracking as it withdrew its extremities from the rear chambers. The torsos on its back began to stir. Beady eyes blinked. Clawed hands quivered. Heads swiveled, searching for the source of the voice.

"Hilt?" she shouted again. Her voice carried through the passageway remarkably well. Hilt could faintly hear Yntri clicking, warning her not to enter the cave. "You had better be alive in there!"

Hilt swore under his breath. He had no choice. He had to leave.

He bit his lip and twirled his swords. But before leaving, he had to try an attack. He had to see what would happen. Hilt called to the magic within his swords, then darted forward around the edge of the bubbling pool and unleashed a powerful double slash, extending the blades of air out past his swords as far as he could. Two very deep slits appeared in its glistening back.

The wounds split open and a dozen clawed arms and torsos reached out, screeching and clawing. Then pushing past them came a large set of curved teeth that opened into a mouth wide enough to swallow him whole. A long tongue uncoiled from within and began reaching and searching for him.

"Hilt if you don't come out of there this instant, I am coming in after you!" came Beth's voice. "I am counting to five!"

Long clawed barbs burst from the end of the tongue and it whipped about wildly, smacking against the floor and ceiling of the cavern, but not coming close to reaching him.

A half dozen small spherical bulges appeared around the gaping mouth, then spit open to reveal large lidless eyes. It saw him now. The tongue stopped its blind searching, and the bulk of the behemoth surged forward, filling the cavern. Hilt smiled. Now this was a beast of legend.

"One!" Beth shouted. Yntri's clicks were getting more plaintive now.

Hilt fumed. Why couldn't she leave him be? Hilt took a half step back and calculated how much damage he could inflict upon the beast before she came in after him.

"Two!"

He took several more steps back, staying just out of its reach. Of course he couldn't cause any significant damage to it without attempting some truly devastating attacks. There were things he might be able to do, but . . . the truth was that he didn't know if he could attempt it without pulling the cave walls down on top of him.

"Three! Hilt, you better-! Hey! Don't you dare touch me again, elf!"

Hilt bit his lip again. But what an opportunity! When would he get the chance to try his skill against such a beast again? He twirled his swords and called to the magic, but hesitated. Would Beth truly be so crazy as to follow through with her threat? Surely she was bluffing.

"Four!" There was no hesitation in her voice and Yntri had stopped trying to convince her. The stubborn woman was going to barge in and Hilt knew there was no way he could protect her against this beast, not in close quarters like this. Then he remembered the half-troll he had left in the outer chamber. She would be forced to face it and the only weapon he had given her was the fire stick.

"Stop your count, I'm coming!" he shouted.

"You'd better! I am going to count to three, and if you aren't out here-!"

"Shut up, woman! I'm coming!"

The behemoth surged forward and its tongue whipped at him again. One quick slice of Northwind lopped off the barbed tip and Hilt backed up to the passageway that lead back to the entrance.

The behemoth slid to the right and shivered as it pulled an enormous tentacle out of one of the side passages. It swung the tentacle towards him and Hilt's eyes widened. This wasn't a tentacle; it was an arm. An arm made of hundreds of troll arms fused together, all of them reaching and grasping.

He backed into the passageway, sliding and nearly stumbling, but he didn't dare turn around. The behemoth's arm followed him into the passageway and he could see that between each set of grasping arms was a toothy mouth opening and closing. This was how it fed. Hilt could imagine the behemoth's hungry arm clearing passageways of screeching rodents. He worked his swords with a blur, sending tiny blades of air magic into the passageway, lopping off hands and arms and cutting mouths in two.

The slimy bulk of the behemoth's arm stopped its pursuit, wedged in the narrow space of the passage. He backed into the outer chamber and almost stumbled over the troll torso he had disabled earlier. Its arms were moving about sluggishly, its head already stitching itself back together.

Hilt lopped the head off, no longer caring if he was just making more trolls. The bright light of day stung his eyes. Wincing, he stormed out of the cave.

Beth stood a ways up the slope to the right of the cave entrance, glaring as he approached. In one hand she held a dry pine branch. In the other she held his fire stick. The cap was off. Yntri stood at her side, Beth's dead viper draped around his shoulders like a reptilian scarf.

"I told you to wait for me down the slope!" Hilt barked.

"And let you charge in to your death?" Beth asked incredulously. "There was no way I was letting you be that stupid."

"And you!" Hilt jabbed a finger at Yntri Yni. "Why didn't you stop her?"

"You think he could?" Beth said.

The elf shrugged and clicked helplessly. Hilt couldn't be

angry with him. There was no stopping Beth if she was determined.

"Well look at me. I'm fine. Not dead! Not even a scratch. I was sneaking up on it. All you did was get its attention."

Beth's glare faltered. "Oh, well-."

"Look, just stay out here and give me a few minutes. I'm going to go back in. There's something I want to try."

"You're not going back in there." Beth said matter-of-factly "You promised to escort me to the top of this mountain."

Hilt grabbed his hair in frustration. "And I will. But first I need to go back and-."

"No," Beth rubbed the end of the fire stick against the dry branch in her other hand.

Hilt threw out his hand in warning, but she didn't give him a chance. Beth tossed the burning branch onto the nearest slime trail. A line of fire streaked towards the cave entrance lighting every trail it crossed.

Wasting no time, Hilt ran to Beth and tossed her over his shoulder, then turned and ran away from the cave. "Yntri!" he yelled, but the elf was already running ahead of them.

When the line of fire hit the pool of slime at the mouth of the cave, there was a whoosh and then a sharp crack. Hilt was knocked from his feet by the concussive blast. His chest struck the ground and Beth tumbled away from him, rolling across the rock.

IV

Hilt's ears rang and as he gasped for air, he looked back to see an enormous twisting plume of flame roaring from the cave entrance. Troll trails everywhere had been lit and the entire ridgeline was aflame. It was sheer luck that the blast had not knocked them into one of those flaming areas or tossed them down the mountainside. Even so, the heat was so oppressive that he feared his clothing would combust. He crawled to Beth.

She was moaning softly. Her left arm had fallen across a lit troll trail and she hadn't yet noticed that the sleeve of her dress had caught fire. He beat out the flames and dragged her to her feet. He grabbed her arm and pulled her further away from the blaze. She staggered along in a daze at first, bruised up and moaning. Then the behemoth's pained roar echoed from the inferno behind them. She forgot about her discomfort and began to jog beside him.

They didn't turn back until the air cooled and they caught up to Yntri. The elf stood with arms folded watching the blaze, the flames reflecting in his squinting eyes. Hilt glanced back over his shoulder. The fire still poured from the cave mouth, flowing upward into the sky like an upside down waterfall. Hilt released Beth's arm and looked her over to make sure she was okay. She was bumped up and bruised and her dress had torn in a few places, but from the way she glared back at him, he figured that she had recovered from her tumble.

"What on earth were you thinking?" Hilt snapped. "We could have all been killed!"

"I made sure we were standing in an area clear of slime

before I lit the trails," she said. "The fire was a bit more intense than I figured though."

"A bit?" Hilt said in disbelief. "And where is my fire stick? Please don't tell me you dropped it."

"Here," she said and stuck out her right hand which was still clenched around the stick, her knuckles white. "I made sure not to let go of it."

"And the cap?" Hilt asked. "Please tell me you didn't lose it."

"Uhh . . ." Her brow furrowed, her eyes darting back and forth for a moment as she tried to remember what she had done with it. Then she sighed in relief. "That's right. Yntri pulled it off when he tried to take the stick away from me."

Hilt glanced over to Yntri. The elf handed it to him wordlessly. Hilt snatched the fire stick from her hand and placed the cap back on it before tucking it into his pocket. "I see that you can't be trusted with this."

"I can't be trusted?" she scoffed. "After you ran off to your doom, leaving me alone with a handsy old elf, I'm the one who can't be trusted?"

Yntri nodded and clicked at Hilt in agreement.

"Look, you two," Hilt said. "I was not going to my doom. I was just checking things out. I wanted to see it."

"And how did that go?"

"It was . . . large," Hilt said.

"Could you have killed it?" she asked, hands on hips.

"Well . . . likely not, but we will never know, will we? You took that opportunity away!"

"It was for your own good!" Beth said. "Why on earth were you so determined to face that thing?"

Hilt clenched his jaw. "It was a matter of-."

"Pride?" she scoffed. "More like a matter of stupidity."

"Yes, pride!" Hilt shouted. He raised his right fist and shook his rune at her. "I was named nearly twenty years ago!

Twenty years since I received the highest honor a warrior can get. It took immense focus and drive to reach those heights, but what then? Where does a driven man go once he's reached the top? Tell me! Where?"

Her jaw hung open in surprise at the intensity of his reaction and she stammered as she tried to find an answer. Yntri clicked a few times and placed a calming hand on Hilt's arm, but the warrior shook him off.

"I'll tell you where," he said. "Once you have reached the peak, there is no direction to go but down."

Beth swallowed. "N-now if you're at the top there's no reason you have to go anywhere . . . is there?"

Hilt laughed, but there was no humor in his voice. "Yes, I suppose I could stand still, poised on my peak, trying to maintain myself. That's what people expect a named warrior to do. And don't get me wrong, for many years I have been content to do so, but lately more and more I get that itch, that need to achieve something again. The monsters of legend are one of the few challenges still out there, one of the few ways I can still improve.

"I already slew one of them." He jerked a thumb at Yntri. "It was the day Yntri and I met. A nightbeast had been haunting one of the villages in Malaroo down by the Jharro grove."

Yntri's brow furrowed. He clicked at Hilt with a scolding tone, jabbing a finger in his direction.

"Yes, I know." Hilt shook his head with a snort. "He tried to warn me off back then too. Yntri likes to tell me my pride is going to kill me some day. I disagree. I think it's what keeps me alive. I was unhappy for a long time before that battle. But when I killed that nightbeast things changed. The Roo-tan welcomed me in. Their leader took my council and started opening up their borders to Dremaldria. That fight changed their country and my life for the better."

His explanation didn't get the response he had hoped for. Beth's look of surprise had turned into a scowl. "So that's what this pride of yours is? A need for fame and glory? You reach the top and that's not good enough for you? You need to keep waving and shouting, 'Look at me! I'm Sir Hilt and I killed stuff, so I'm still the greatest!'"

"Stuff?" Now it was Hilt's turn to stammer. "Y-you think this is about fame? You think that if I had killed that behemoth, word of my victory would spread? You think bards would travel around singing about it? How? No one knows it's here!"

"Oh, and you wouldn't tell anyone about it? Sure." Beth rolled her eyes. "Who needs a bard when you can sing your own praises?"

"Had you ever heard of me before today, Beth?" When she didn't answer right away, Hilt nodded in satisfaction. "You don't know a fraction of the things I've done. No one does. I don't seek out the praise of others. Praise comes on its own sometimes when you do good works, but that's not why I do what I do. This is *my* pride. It's about me."

"All about you?" Beth's scowl hadn't faded. "So you're admitting that you're selfish. You go around pretending to want to help, but when it comes down to it, you'll put your stupid pride above everyone else."

Hilts face went red with indignation, but Beth didn't back down. Yntri clicked and whistled soothingly and took a step between them in an attempt to calm things down, but they just ignored the elf, glaring around him.

Hilt's fists shook. "It's . . . You . . . You're just determined to antagonize me, aren't you?"

Beth threw up her hands. "What's going to happen next time, hmm? If we get near the top of this mountain and we need your help, but the world's largest squirrel runs by, are you going to leave us and run off chasing it? Huh, mister selfish?"

They leaned in close, eyes locked, matching each other glare for glare for several seconds, Yntri stuck uncomfortably between them. Then Hilt's lips twitched. Beth's glare faltered. Both of them burst into laughter.

Yntri watched their mirth, confusion etched on his wrinkled face. He scratched his head and clicked a wary question.

"Yes! Yes, Yntri, I suppose we are crazy. " Hilt laughed some more. He shook his head at Beth. "World's largest squirrel? Really?"

"It's what popped into my mind at the time," Beth said, holding her bruised sides and wincing. "I know it doesn't sound very dangerous, but the picture I had of it in my mind had really sharp teeth."

As the laughter died down, Hilt shook his head. "Beth and Yntri . . . you were both right. I have two missions ahead of me and I put both of them in jeopardy by chasing after the behemoth. That was indeed . . . selfish of me and inexcusable behavior. I am very sorry."

Beth looked quite surprised that he had admitted it. "I forgive you. And I-I apologize for antagonizing you . . . and for almost blowing all of us up."

Hilt gave her a sincere bow. "I am most grateful for your forgiveness and I accept your sincere apology. What about you, Yntri? Do you forgive us?"

The elf shrugged and clicked a few times, then turned and hiked on, talking back to Hilt over his shoulder.

"Yntri says it is getting late." The sun had indeed nearly reached the horizon. Clouds at the edges of the skyline had begun to turn a pink hue. "We should find a good place to stop for the night. Can you climb a bit further?"

Beth nodded, though she looked exhausted. Hilt didn't blame her for being tired. It was hard to believe that their climb had just begun that morning. They had been through a lot in that short period of time.

They followed Yntri up the slope in silence for a while. Hilt kept an eye on the woman, making sure she was holding up alright. Beth's movements were a bit labored as she trudged on. He wondered if her fall had done more than just bruised her. Despite obvious discomfort, Beth didn't complain.

When she did speak again, her look was introspective. "Hilt . . . when you were in the cave . . ."

"Yes?" he said.

Her head was down and her voice hesitant as she added, "The beast. What did it look like?"

Hilt noted the fear in her posture and replied, "A nightmare. You don't want to know."

She nodded, then asked a few seconds later, "Do you think that the fire killed it?"

Yntri, who was just a few yards ahead of them laughed and clicked back at her.

"He says that if fire killed it the behemoth wouldn't be a legend," Hilt translated. "He's right. Troll behemoths heal too quickly even for fire. Perhaps if one was starved and then you set it on fire . . ."

She eyed him with suspicion. "You are thinking about strategies in case you decide to come back and face it later, aren't you?"

Hilt chuckled. "Already you know me so well. But don't worry. I will see you to the top of this mountain. Then I have another mission to finish before I can even think of coming back."

That didn't seem to make her feel better. She folded her arms. "I really had hoped I'd killed it."

"If it is any consolation, that inferno doubtless caused the deaths of hundreds of trolls that were growing from its side. They hung from its back like bunches of grapes." She grimaced and he added, "Come to think of it, you probably killed the population of rodents that it was feeding off in there. It's too large to leave that cave and without a food source, it may starve to death. So oddly enough, your fire may kill the beast after all. Imagine that! Beth, killer of legends!"

A slight smile reached her lips at that thought and she straightened up a bit, but Yntri shook his head and clicked again.

"Oh," Hilt said as the elf continued on.

"What was it?" she asked.

"Evidently the rodents weren't its only food source. Yntri says that there is another entrance to the cave on further down the mountain." Yntri clicked some more. "Ah, more like a shaft, really. There is a tribe of orcs living there that worship the thing. Evidently they've been sacrificing to it. Yntri saw them throw a deer down the shaft on the way up here. It wasn't until he reached the cave mouth that he realized what they were feeding."

Beth slumped again. "Well good for you then, Sir Hilt. There is still a chance for you to exercise your pride in the future."

Hilt forced himself not to respond. He had argued enough with the woman for one day. He didn't understand why she was so quick to anger, but he couldn't help but respect her fortitude. It suddenly struck him how brave of her it had been to climb to the top of the ridge and stand before the behemoth's cave to call him out. She had been so shaken by her fear of trolls and yet had stood there with fire stick in hand, determined to save his life.

He placed a hand on her shoulder. "Thank you Beth for coming after me. I know it wasn't an easy thing to do."

Her eye brows rose in surprise and she gave him a tired smile. "How was I going to reach the top without you?"

Yntri called out to them and pointed.

"What is it?" Hilt looked over at him and nodded. "Well it seems he's found us a place to camp for the evening."

The elf had found a stand of trees that were butted up against a jutting rock shelf. The location provided a shelter from wind and a place where they could build a small cookfire that wouldn't be easily seen. In addition, there were no signs of trolls or other monsters nearby that could provide a threat.

To Hilt's surprise, someone had used this spot to camp before and not long ago. There was a small ring of blackened soil under the overhanging rock where someone had built a fire and the area had been swept mostly clear of pine needles. Gorcs and orcs tended to leave their camping spots in disarray, so it was likely the previous occupant had been a human.

It wasn't a heavily wooded area, but he and Beth were able to go around to several nearby tree clusters and break off dead limbs and sticks, gathering dry wood for the cookfire. Hilt was getting hungry enough that even the thought of eating viper sounded good.

"So Hilt," Beth said, her arms full of sticks and branches. "You haven't told me why you and Yntri were out here in Renuel. Malaroo is quite a journey from here."

"Oh, well Xedrion Bin Leeths, the current leader of the Roo-tan, wanted someone to talk his daughter into coming home. It was time for Yntri's yearly pilgrimage and it had been years since I had seen the academy, so we agreed to go." Hilt explained. "As you can see, we are returning empty handed."

"Really? A Roo-tan princess refused to come home and you just let her?"

Hilt laughed. "If you had met her you wouldn't be surprised. Her name is Jhonate and she's even more stubborn than you, if you can believe a woman like that exists. But she's not a princess in the way you would think. She's not an heir to the Roo-tan or anything. However, she is one of her father's favorites and she wasn't supposed to have left the country."

Beth shook her head. "What was she doing in Reneul then?"

"Ah, well it is partially my fault to tell the truth. Her father had just opened up trade with Dremaldria and I was regaling the children with stories of the Battle Academy. I bragged that it was the greatest warrior school in the known lands and I told Xedrion that his people could benefit by having a relationship with the academy. He agreed that it would be a good idea and the next day Jhonate disappeared. He received a note from her a week later saying that she was traveling to the academy as his representative."

"He must have been furious," Beth said in amusement.

"Extremely," Hilt said. "He sent two trackers after her but they failed to bring her back. It was quite an embarrassing situation for him and his opponents in the kingdom got a good laugh out of it. Several months later, he received a letter from the academy thanking him for sending his envoy and saying that they had accepted her for entrance into the school and included a glowing review from Faldon the Fierce himself, praising her prowess."

She raised her eyebrows. "Really? She got in that quickly?"

"Evidently she came to the gates of the school, gave them my name as reference, and presented herself as an official envoy of the Roo-tan sent to study at the academy. Usually applicants of the academy have to take training school for a year, but due to her diplomatic status and battle prowess they let her in right away. Xedrion was angry, but he couldn't help but be proud of her accomplishment and his hands were tied since the academy had been so gracious. So he put up with it. But after a year went by, he changed his mind. He figured that he had left her there long enough to show the academy respect, so he sent us to retrieve her."

They returned to the campsite with all the wood they could carry. Yntri wasn't there and Hilt figured the elf had gone hunting. The sun had disappeared beyond the horizon and light was quickly fading so he got a fire started with his fire stick. They huddled around the small fire and enjoyed the warmth as they waited for Yntri's return.

"So what happened when you got to Reneul?" Beth asked. "I mean, obviously the girl refused to return home, but why?"

"Jhonate was always an impetuous child much like Xedrion himself had been. It was one of the reasons he doted on her. But in Malaroo, no matter how much she excelled, she was always seen by the people as the least of her siblings and she found that unacceptable. At the academy, however, your order of birth doesn't matter. Every student there is given all the respect they earn and that fits perfect with her sensibilities. She was happy there and Xedrion knew it. So when we left, he sent us with some heavy . . . incentives."

"What was going to convince her?" Beth leaned in close to him as they talked and Hilt could tell she was getting cold. He took off his overcoat and slid it across her shoulders.

"Xedrion understood her reasons for leaving and had come up with a way to raise her esteem among her peers. I told you about Yntri's bow earlier, how it is made of living Jharro wood. Well Jhonate already had one Jharro weapon, all the good warriors among her people have one. However Xedrion asked Yntri to make her another one. That is a rare honor among their people. Only Xedrion's own elite force has two Jharro weapons and only her eldest brother was good enough to be counted among those elite.

"So Yntri made her a Jharro bow and her father included a golden dragon hair bowstring, a priceless prize in and of itself. If Jhonate returned to her people with two Jharro weapons, the golden bowstring, and the training of the Battle Academy she would have all the respect she could ever want. Yntri was going to present the weapon to her himself and I came along to smooth things over with the academy and make sure that there were no hard feelings left behind. I was authorized to set up a warrior exchange program where the top students from the school would be allowed to come and train with the Roo-tan for a while, Xedrion had even agreed to open his kingdom to academy contracts."

"And she refused all that?" Beth asked in amazement, clutching his coat close around her.

"Well, things didn't go as planned. You see, she had been doing so well that Faldon the Fierce had offered her a one year contract, paying her to train his son, who was struggling to pass the tests necessary to enter the academy. She was all but ready to return with us, however the Roo-tan take contracts very seriously. Her year was almost up when we arrived and we decided to wait for her to complete it.

"But then she took Yntri to check out her student, who was struggling with the bow. He's the other person Yntri met this year with talent like yours. The boy was just too stubborn to listen to his archery instructor. This is when things went wrong. The bow that Yntri had brought intending to give it to Jhonate, bonded to her student instead. And when a Jharro weapon bonds to someone it is permanent."

"Oh my," Beth said.

"It wasn't supposed to be possible," Hilt said as he fed a few more sticks to the fire. "There is usually a whole ceremony involved. Before a warrior is given a weapon, he spends a night sleeping in the boughs of the host tree before it gives up the wood.

Jhonate had already done so as a child, but her student had never seen a Jharro tree.

"Yhtri thinks it was because he spent so much time in contact with Jhonate's weapon. Since both came from the same tree, it recognized him. Regardless, we could no longer use it as an incentive to bring her home. Yntri gave Jhonate permission to give it to her student and she gave it to him on his birthday, golden string and all.

"At that point Yntri continued on his pilgrimage and I stayed behind, hoping that I could still convince her to return to her father. I worked out the details of Xedrion's agreement with the academy and even helped Jhonate train her student. I must admit, he wasn't a natural with the sword, but he impressed me with his determination."

Hilt shrugged. "Anyway Yntri returned just a few days early from his pilgrimage with news of problems with the Jharro grove. Xedrion wanted us to return right away."

"So she decided to stay behind?" Beth asked

"Most likely." Hilt said. "When we left, she was still unsure whether or not she was going to return, but I bet she stays. Yntri can still provide her a new weapon when she comes back and make good on her father's offer, but her heart seems to be with the academy. She really wants to graduate and feels that by doing so, she will forge a stronger bond between the academy and the Roo-tan. I can't really disagree with her there."

There was a whistle from the trees and Yntri entered the campsite clicking happily. The elf held out two rock squirrels that he had shot. He was also dragging a sapling that he had cut down somewhere along the way.

"So we are adding squirrel to our meal tonight?" Beth asked with a smile.

Yntri clicked and Hilt chuckled, "He says they may not be the world's largest, but they will have to do."

"Good!" Beth said. "I was wondering how we were going to get by on one snake split three ways."

Yntri held out Beth's snake and asked a question, pointing at the head.

"He wants to know if he can keep the head," Hilt said. "He has a use for the venom."

"Uh, sure," she said, then added with a hesitant smile, "And Hilt, what I said earlier about cooking the snake? I am a good cook, really I am, but don't be too disappointed if it doesn't come out like I promised. I don't really have the means with me to cook it the way I usually do. I mean, I would bake it in my oven at home with garlic and butter, but I have none of that with me now."

"Don't worry," Hilt said with a reassuring smile. "Yntri makes for a great travel companion. He holds his own in a fight, he's not too talkative, he cleans up after himself, and he's a pretty good cook as well, you'll see."

Yntri unstrung his bow, grabbed the smooth grey wood and twisted. A section of the bow came off and changed in his hands, taking the shape of a knife. He began gutting and skinning his catch. He laid the carcasses out on their skins, then carefully removed the viper's head and skinned it as well.

The elf opened his small pack and pulled out two pouches, one containing ground salt and the other filled with dried leaves. He rubbed both salt and herbs into the meat and skewered both squirrels on a sharpened stick. He then wrapped the viper meat around them and hung the laden skewer between two y-shaped sticks he had planted on either side of the rock circle. The elf squatted by his newly made spit and slowly turned the meat over the fire.

Yntri looked at Beth and clicked a long question, curiosity in his ancient eyes.

"Good question," Hilt said, echoing the elf's expression with his own eyes. "Why are you on this mountain?"

"Because the Prophet told me to."

"We know that part," Hilt said. "Would you mind telling us the rest?"

Beth looked back and forth between them and swallowed.

"That . . . is a long story."

"I told you my long story earlier," Hilt said. "Your turn."

Beth looked at the two of them and hesitated. She didn't tell people about her past. Every question would just lead to more questions and . . . she just didn't want to relive it all again. However, Hilt had risked his life several times to save her and whether she had wanted his help or not, he had earned her trust.

"Okay, I'll tell you, but I need to sit down." She didn't add that her feet hurt, her back hurt, she had a headache, and she was pretty sure that her entire left side was one massive bruise from when Hilt had dropped her. But she never had been a complainer. She had left that to her mother.

"Here," Hilt said. He opened his pack and pulled out a small bundle of pink cloth about the size of a handkerchief.

"I'm supposed to sit on that?" Beth asked. Hilt chuckled. He was so quick to laugh. It reminded her a bit of her husband. "No. But it should keep you warm."

He unfolded it and kept unfolding it. The cloth was thin and gauzy and by the time he was done it was the size of a large bed sheet.

"That's supposed to keep me warm?" The pink thing fluttered in the breeze and if he let it go, she imagined it would soar off into the sky.

Hilt sighed and gave her that patient look she found so infuriating in men. "It's elf made. Despite how it looks, this blanket filters out the cold. Don't ask me how it works, but it keeps you warm even when it's wet. Here try it."

He handed it to her and as she wrapped it around herself, she got goose bumps. It was as if she had wrapped herself in a warm room. She could still feel the night breeze but for some reason when it passed through the fabric, all the cold was taken out of it. She looked closer at the fabric and switched to mage sight. Her vision shifted and she saw a deep black pattern of earth magic woven into the fibers of the blanket interspersed with tiny flecks of gold.

"Yntri, did your people make this?" she asked.

The elf clicked dismissively.

"It doesn't get cold in the Jharro groves," Hilt explained. "No this was a gift from the Blotland elves. It was given to me the last time I went on one of the Prophet's errands."

"Why didn't you just get this out in the first place instead of giving me your jacket? You have got to be freezing right now." Beth scolded. She shrugged out of Hilt's overcoat and handed it to him.

Hilt just shrugged and put his coat back on. "That blanket is very valuable. I didn't want it burnt by the fire."

He sounded sincere, but she knew it was more than that. After all, it was a more chivalrous gesture for a man to offer a lady his coat. Hilt couldn't resist a bit of chivalry. It was a trait she found both charming and annoying in equal measure.

"So why the pink?" she asked, holding the fabric out. It wasn't exactly a color she imagined the swordsman picking out.

Hilt gave her a flat look. "It was brown when the elves gave it to me, but it turned pink the first time I washed it. I think it was their idea of a joke. The Blotland Elves despise the other races, no matter how helpful we try to be."

Yntri laughed and nodded.

"Well I think it's quite pretty," she teased.

Hilt put one hand over his face. "Don't you have a story to tell?"

"Right," Beth sat down with the blanket draped over her and began, "Well . . . I'm not really from Pinewood. I mean, I am. Just not originally. I'm from Dremald. My father was a merchant and though he and my mother had come from a poor family, father had a way with money. He became very wealthy, but not well respected. Father was obsessed with respect. His greatest dream was to become nobility. He tried every scheme he could think of: kissing up to the nobles, bribing officials, under the table deals, but there was no way they were letting him in."

"It would take an appointment by the king," Hilt said. "Dremaldria hasn't had a new noble family in centuries. Either that or-."

"Marry into one of the families, yes." Beth finished. "When I was fifteen, my parents started bringing around suitors. They were minor sons of minor houses, mainly. Pale, stork necked boys, whose parents were running low on money. Marrying me wouldn't bring noble families any prestige, but it would definitely bring a handsome dowry.

"But I wanted nothing to do with that. I didn't care about wealth or prestige. I didn't want some noble boy. I was only interested in one boy. His name was Coulton and he was poorer than dirt. He's the one who taught me the bow. Or at least he was the one that introduced me to it. I saw him shooting with some friends one day and he let me try. It came naturally to me. It was like the center of the target called out to my arrows. I bought some nice bows and whenever my parents weren't looking, I'd sneak out and shoot with him.

"I was able to keep it secret for a while, but then one day my mother was driving by in her carriage. She saw me with him shooting and got angry. I told her that he was only a friend and it was just about the bow. And it was! Or at least at first, it had been about the bow, but she had seen Coulton with his arm around me, helping me aim and-."

Yntri laughed and shook his head, clicking something as he turned the meat on the spit. Hilt nodded, but didn't translate right away.

"What did he say?" she asked with suspicion.

"Oh, uh. He said that you didn't need help," Hilt said. She narrowed his eyes at him and he added, "And then he said, 'lucky boy'."

"Well, it's true that I was a better shot than he was," she admitted. "And I did enjoy letting him think he was helping. Coulton was such a sweet boy and charming. He had this laugh . . ." She realized that she was smiling wistfully and paused to clear her throat. "Anyway, it was over after that. Mother hauled me home and forbid me to see him again. Father paid a guard to follow me around."

"Don't tell me that worked." Hilt said with a smile.

Why did it seem like he knew her so well? "I was pretty determined. I escaped from my 'guard' a few times, but no matter where I looked, I couldn't find Coulton again. No one knew where he was, not even his friends. A few weeks later my parents found the suitor they liked best. His name was Huber and he was the son of Duke Karl Wolden."

"Ah, the Woldens," Hilt said. His voice carried a sympathetic tone. "Such a boring lot. One of the oldest families and one of the poorest. Not that they acknowledge it. They spend so much time focused on their past that they ignore the present. I had to go to Wolden parties often as a child. Lavish monstrosities."

"That describes them perfectly," she agreed. "It was the match my father had been waiting for. He needed a noble son. They needed to replenish their coffers. A marriage deal was struck. The date was set for the week after my sixteenth birthday.

"I couldn't stand Huber, though honestly it wasn't his fault. He was polite enough and better looking than half the other suitors my parents had dragged me to see. He was just dull like the rest of his family. Oh, I was so mean to him. By the time my birthday came, he was terrified. I hoped that he would convince his family to call it off, but both our parents were determined. To this day I have no idea what father promised them."

Hilts eyebrows were raised. "So how did you escape that trap? Or didn't you? Should I go back to calling you my lady?"

She glowered at him. "I was saved by magic."

V

Yntri clicked and whistled, interrupting the story. He gestured at the meat on the spit. The snake was a golden brown on the edges and the bits of fat in the squirrel meat popped and sizzled as it dripped into the fire.

"Time to eat," Hilt said.

Beth was famished and the smell had been making her mouth water for a while. The herbs the elf had rubbed into the meat had a savory aroma. The three of them stood around the spit and pulled pieces of meat off of the spit, careful not to drop any into the fire. The meat was hot and Beth burned her fingers a few times as she tucked it into her mouth, but she didn't care. The flavor of the herb Yntri had used was different than she had expected, both salty and sweet and slightly bitter. Mixed with the flavor of the meat, it was heavenly.

Once they were finished, Beth sucked the grease from her fingers feeling happy, though a bit disappointed that there wasn't more. As she looked into the eyes of her companions, though, her mood faded. The two men were curious, waiting for her to continue her story. She began to feel panic bubble up inside her. There were parts of this story she had never told anyone and there were parts of this story that could very well change their opinion of her. She began to feel a bit queasy.

"Are you okay?" Hilt asked, his face etched in concern.

"I . . . I can't tell this story without something in my hands . . . Just, um . . . I know what I can do. Turn around for a second, will you?" Hilt dutifully obeyed but Yntri just watched her expectantly. She frowned. "You too, Yntri."

The elf shrugged and turned around.

Beth untied the leather strips binding the split halves of her dress to her legs and tucked the edge of the blanket under her chin while she undid the buttons on her dress, keeping an eye on the men as she did so. She trusted Hilt not to turn back around, but the elf on the other hand was iffy. Once she had removed the torn and soiled dress, she stood in her undershirt and short hose and wrapped the elven blanket around herself, tucking it under her arms.

"Okay, you're fine now," Beth said and the two men turned back around.

"What are you doing?" Hilt asked. Yntri just shrugged and went back to sucking the marrow from the squirrel bones.

"I . . ." Beth shook out the dress and reached into her pocket, pulling out her needle and thread. "Am doing some alterations."

She sat down and began lining up the small tears in the arms and bodice from her tumbles during the day. It looked like she had just enough thread to do what she planned. She began sewing up the holes with short practiced strokes. The familiar repetitiveness of the needlework helped her put her mind in order and she felt the tension drain away. "Ugh, this thing is filthy. I wish I had a way to clean it."

"You were telling us your story," Hilt reminded.

"Right," she said, continuing to stitch as she talked. "The week of my wedding, Huber's family threw a series of ridiculous parties, bankrolled by my father, I'm sure. One of them was a traveling menagerie run by some beardless dwarves with odd accents. It was a stunning display. Exotic colorful animals I have never heard of, acrobats, stunts-."

"The Dwarf Rider Menagerie," Hilt said. "I saw them once as a child. I was awestruck by it all, but my father told me that they were just smugglers masquerading as a legitimate business."

"Well I was fascinated," she said. "The last act was billed as a display of the most dangerous animals in the known lands.

They started bringing out cages filled with poisonous snakes, huge spiders, bears, enormous mountain cats . . . Something strange began to happen to me. I-I looked at these creatures and saw their minds. They were scared. They were trapped and hungry and didn't understand the sounds and smells of the hundreds of humans around them.

"The next thing I knew, people were screaming. Rough voices were shouting at me. I was standing in the middle of the cages with my arms wrapped around the neck of a huge treecat. The beast was at least three times my size, yet I was scratching it behind the ears like a kitten.

"These angry dwarves dragged me away from the beast and locked it back in its cage. I was stunned. I don't remember leaving my seat, don't remember walking into the center of the menagerie, and I definitely do not remember opening the treecat's cage. The dwarves told my parents that I was lucky to be alive. They said that particular treecat was a vile beast with a known taste for human flesh.

"That night wizards from the Mage School knocked at my parent's door. They called what had happened an awakening, that I was the right age for it to happen, and that I was to be taken to the Mage School to learn to control my magic."

"Amazing," Hilt said. "I have never heard of a wizard with the ability to control animals."

"Neither had they. They told me that awakenings were strange and instinctual, that wizards are often not able to duplicate what they had done the day their powers revealed themselves. When it comes to calming animals, it's something I've always been able to do, but then again it was never something I had control over. It just happens."

"How did your parents react?"

"My parents were devastated. Their plans were ruined and no amount of begging or bribing could get the wizards to change their mind. The wedding was called off. It would take years of training at the school before I could return. To me this was heaven. I was glad to get away from the nobility. My only sadness came from the fact that I had to leave Coulton behind. I didn't even have a way to tell him what had happened."

Beth finished the last stitch on the bodice and flipped the dress around to work on the skirts. She turned it inside out and took up the jagged edges she had made when splitting the skirts with her knife. She started at the bottom and began stitching together a new seam. When she was ready to continue her story, she looked up and noticed Hilt shaking his head in bewilderment.

"What?" she asked.

"All this time, I thought I was escorting a poor housewife, and now I find out that you are a wealthy mage? Couldn't a little magic have helped us somewhere along the way?"

"I'm not finished yet," Beth reminded him. "When I first got to the Mage School, I was amazed by the place. The grounds were beautiful and the teachers amazing. Then they tested my power levels and I was so disappointed. All my elements were pretty low. My strengths were air and fire, but even those were minimal. I soon discovered that my only true strength was in runework. I didn't have much magic of my own, but I had a knack for manipulating magic that was already there."

Yntri clicked and Hilt translated, "He says that is one of the prime qualities of a great archer. Wait, I don't get that Yntri. What does archery have to do with magic?"

The ancient elf explained, using broad gestures with his hands as he spoke.

"Huh," Hilt said. "This is a bit hard to translate, but he says that the best swordsmen are creators at heart, while the best archers are shapers. Did I explain that right, Yntri?"

The elf shrugged and waggled one hand to show that it was close to what he meant.

Beth paused in her stitching. "I don't know that I quite follow, but I think it's a good way to describe me. I was a shaper. I got better at it the longer I was there. A few years later I became an apprentice. My master was a stern woman, but kind and very enthusiastic about my potential.

"Then one day not long after I turned twenty, I was put on a new project. The council had decided to add another wing to the testing center at the school. I was one of the students adding runework to the new walls to strengthen them. One day while I was working, someone tapped me on the shoulder and when I turned around, I about died. It was Coulton.

"He had heard where I was and had hired on with the laborers brought in to help. At first I was furious at him for disappearing on me, but it turned out that it wasn't his fault."

"Your father?" Hilt asked. "My father did that to my brother once. He got too fond of one of our scullery maids and father had her shipped off to another nobleman."

"My mother," Beth said. "But worse. She had him jailed. They never even told him why. He sat in the dungeons for a year before they let him out. He came looking for me, but my parents had moved to another part of Dremald. Eventually he found out what had happened to me and spent a long time searching for a way to see me. The Mage School limits visitors to family members and even that's a rarity, so it wasn't possible."

"He couldn't have sent you a message?" Hilt asked.

"He didn't know how to write," Beth said. "At any rate, the building project only lasted three weeks. We saw each other as much as we could, but when it came time for him to leave, I didn't want him to go. When I told him so, he told me he loved me. He told me he was willing to wait for me until I left the school. But that would take too long. It would be years until I would have the freedom to leave.

"I couldn't stand being away from him again. I went to my master and asked her to plead my case before the council, but their rules were firm. Coulton could not stay at the school and they would not allow me to leave. There was only one choice left to me . . ."

Hilts jaw tightened in understanding. "They quelled you."

"It was my decision," she said. "Their rules, but my decision."

Students in the Mage School were not allowed to leave until they had at least become mages, fully aware of their abilities and the responsibilities that came with them. If a student wanted to leave before they were deemed ready, there was only one option; to voluntarily have their magical abilities ripped from them. It was offered as a merciful option, but Quelling was permanent and only used otherwise as a punishment to dangerous wizards gone mad with power. The rule had existed from the beginning of the Mage School and perhaps of all the rules, this was the most controversial.

Yntri clicked a question.

"He wants to know if it hurt," Hilt said.

Beth nodded, biting her lip. "They warn you all about it before they let you make the decision. The pain was bad, but perhaps the cruelest part is that even after being quelled, your mage sight still works. M-my magic is gone, but I can still see the magic in the world around me. I can see it but I can't touch it. Imagine this, Sir Hilt. What if your ability to fight was taken away? What if you could see your swords, but whenever the time came to use them, you had no way to pick them up? That's what it's like."

"I am sorry," Hilt said, meeting her gaze with genuine sadness in his eyes.

Beth felt tears beginning to well up at his kind sentiment and it made her angry. How dare he make her cry? She swallowed the tears away. Why cry for this? This was old news. Worse things had happened since.

"Oh, it's all right. I was stupid and stubborn and I paid for it. I spent a day recuperating and then they released me. Coulton and I left the Mage School and got married in Sampo. After that, we traveled for a while. I took up the bow again. It felt good to have that skill with something. For a while we used it to make money. We'd come upon a group of tough men with bows and Coulton had this line he'd use." She smiled at the memory. "He'd say, 'You don't look so great. Even my wife could beat you.' Most fools couldn't resist that. They'd accept the challenge and I'd win."

"That must have made them angry," Hilt said.

"Oh yes. They would usually pay up at first, if just to save face with their friends, but sometimes they would come after us later. We got very good at running and hiding." She sighed. "But it didn't last. We tried it one too many times and word got out. After a few very close calls and after Coulton took one severe beating, I put down my bow. He got a job with a carpenter in Pinewood and that's where we stayed."

"And your parents?" Hilt asked.

"I heard they were looking for me for a while, but I didn't want to see them. Not after what they did to Coulton. Last I knew they were still in Dremald, rich as ever, still scheming for nobility. Ridiculous!"

She finished the last stitch on the inseam of the garment and tied it off. "There, done! Oh, I wish I had some scissors to shorten the legs a bit but this will have to do. Now turn around for a minute you two while I put this on."

Once the men had dutifully obeyed, she unwrapped the blanket from around her and shivered in the cold air as she put her creation on. "Okay, I'm finished. It really isn't made for this, but I stitched it pretty well. It should stay together I think."

"I am quite impressed, actually," Hilt said with an appreciative nod. "I daresay that outfit could be the start of a new fashion trend."

Beth snorted and tied one leather strip around the bottom of each leg, gathering the material together to avoid another snag. "Oh, sure. First, sleep under the leaves for a few days. Second step, fall down a mountain. Then all you have to do is cut your dress in half and sew it back together. This will spread like wild fire."

Hilt chucked, "Say what you will, I think you look charming."

"Charming . . .? You're teasing me, aren't you?"

"Not at all." He smiled at her for a moment, but then his expression turned serious. "Beth, what happened to your husband?"

Beth draped the gauzy blanket back around her shoulders

and stared into the fire. "That's what it comes down to, isn't it? Here I've gone and told you my whole life story just to put off this part . . ."

Hilt folded his arms and gazed into the fire with her. "You don't really have to tell us if you don't want to, Beth. Yntri and I are going to help you finish climbing this mountain tomorrow whether you tell us or not."

Beth blinked and looked at him questioningly. She hadn't expected him to say that. Suddenly it seemed to her as if this was an important moment. She gazed back into the flames and the fire flared. She saw two pathways stretching before her. On one path she stopped her story there and finished her quest the next day, burying her past behind her. That path ended rather abruptly. On the second path, she opened up and told Hilt the rest, reliving the entire horrible truth of it. That path was hazy and had a variety of possible endings she could not see. She waffled back and forth, but finally closed her eyes, cutting off the vision.

"You are risking your lives to help me. You deserve to know the rest." She took a shuddering breath. "Coulton died almost a year ago."

Hilt nodded solemnly. "I'm sorry."

"It was, um . . . an odd month. His father had come to town. Just out of the blue, Coulton's father that had left him when he was just a child showed up and wanted to see him. He told us that he was dying and he wanted to reconcile with his son. Coulton listened to his story and hugged that ragged little man.

"Coulton told me that he wanted to let his father stay with us. He wanted to care for him until he died. I didn't know how to react. I was both repulsed by the idea and more in love with him than ever. If my father had come to me with the same story, I wouldn't have been able to do that." She sighed. "So it was just the three of us for a while."

"Just three of you? What about-."

"No." She shook her head. "We weren't able to have children. Quelling does that sometimes to a woman. It doesn't work that way with men, but . . . they warned me about that too, before I made my decision, so I only have myself to blame."

Yntri frowned and clicked at her as he shook a disapproving finger.

"He says you are blaming yourself too much," Hilt said. "And I agree with him. Quelling is a barbaric tradition. I can't believe they still do it today."

"But it is also necessary," Beth said. "You may not have seen all the things these students could do, how out of control they were. If the Mage School didn't teach them to control their magic and just let them go . . . No, this was my decision. My consequences. If I hadn't been so unwilling to wait a few years, I would still have my magic. I could have had children. I would have made more than enough money as a Mage for us to live differently. Then again, maybe Coulton wouldn't have waited for me. He might have found another woman and had a different life. Either way, he would still be alive. No, this is my fault. Mine! Don't you try to take away my guilt!"

"Beth-." Hilt said, reaching out to her.

"Shut up and let me finish my story!" She snapped. He let his arm fall back to his side and Beth looked back at the fire.

"Things were actually okay with Coulton's father around. His name was Robert, but he told us to call him Old Bob. Old Bob was a sweet man after a fashion. Coulton built him a bed and though it was a tight fit in our little house, we made do.

"Then one evening Coulton didn't come home from work. I went to see his boss and he said that Coulton had gone into the woods looking for some trees to harvest. The next morning we went looking for him and, um . . ." Her voice slipped and her lip quivered. She brought one shaking hand up to wipe her eyes.

"He had been torn apart. Eaten by moonrats. Th-they had been getting more numerous for a while and bolder. More of them had been seen on our side of the road's protective barriers. People had been attacked before, but this was the first time that a Pinewood man had been . . ."

Beth didn't see Hilt approach, but she felt his comforting

hand on her shoulder. She let him leave it there. It actually helped. She cleared her throat.

"I, uh, had nothing left to do. I had no one but Old Bob and I barely knew him. The people of Pinewood were kind to me and helped out as they could. Old Bob's condition got worse until he couldn't get out of bed anymore. He was the only part of Coulton I had left, so I-I stayed by him until the end. The day we buried Old Bob next to Coulton's grave, I left. I just walked into the forest."

"Where were you going?" Hilt asked.

"To die most likely. I headed towards the deepest part of the forest. The darkest part. I went to see if the rumors were true; if the moonrats did have a mother there. If she did exist, I intended to strangle her to death with my bare hands."

"And if she didn't exist?" Hilt asked.

"Then I would start strangling moonrats. The beasts hadn't attacked me in the past, but maybe this time they would. If I died, I would be with Coulton again. If not, I would just keep killing them until there were no moonrats left." She raised one hand to her shoulder and rested it on Hilt's. "But I found the Prophet instead. I walked through the forest until I came upon the Mage School's warded road and he was standing there as if waiting for me."

"What did he say?" Hilt asked.

Though her memory of the Prophet's appearance was fuzzy, Beth could still recall every word of their conversation as if it was burned into her mind. "He said, 'Where are you going?' I said, 'That way.' He said, 'Hello, my name is John.' I had no patience left for pleasantries and said, 'Goodbye, John.' He said, 'That's not where you need to go.' I frowned at him and said, 'How do you know where I need to go?' He said, 'You are looking for answers, but the way you are heading has no answers, only death.' I said, 'What if death is the answer I'm looking for?' He said, 'You don't even know the question yet.'"

"He is annoying that way," Hilt said. "The way he talks in riddles. He's even worse than Yntri." The elf had been nodding in agreement, but stopped and frowned.

"I found him . . . interesting," Beth said with a shrug. "And at that point I hadn't found anyone interesting in a long while. I asked him why I should listen to him and he said, 'I am the Prophet.' For some reason I believed him right away. I had no reason to, but I had no reason not to either. I said, 'Where do I go, then?' He said, 'Walk to the east. On the far side of the woods is a mountain. Climb to the top and you will find the answer you seek.' I said, 'When do I leave?' He said, 'Go now.' and . . ."

She stopped and looked back at Hilt. "I think I already told you the rest."

Yntri clicked a question.

"He asks what gave you so much faith in the Prophet that you would blindly follow such a vague and ridiculous request?" Hilt said. "Actually I added the word ridiculous."

"Faith?" Beth furrowed her brow as if thinking about the word for the first time. Finally she shrugged. "I guess at that point faith was all I had left."

No one said anything for a moment. Beth felt a strange sense of peace come over her and it was as if some of the weight she had been carrying was lifted from her shoulders. She had told her story and neither of them had turned away from her or looked at her in disgust. They hadn't pitied her either. They were just . . . supportive. Beth yawned. Telling the story had taken a lot out of her.

"I'm tired," she said.

"Yes, I suppose we should get some sleep," Hilt agreed. "Tomorrow could be a long day."

Yntri stood and clicked at her for a while before heading to the edge of the campsite. He picked up the sapling he had brought with him earlier and started hacking off the branches.

"What did he say?" Beth asked.

"He said that you are a brave woman," Hilt told her.

"Surely he said more than that." Beth said. The elf had talked for a while.

"If it helps at all, I agree with him," Hilt added, not

answering her question.

She looked at him, trying to decide whether to push the subject. Then she saw Yntri drag the sapling over to one of the trees. The elf climbed up into the tree, taking the sapling up with him.

"What is he doing?" she asked.

"He's taking watch," Hilt said. "He likes taking a perch up in the trees because it gives him a good view of the area all around."

"But those are fir trees and . . . he's practically naked," she said with a shiver. "That can't be comfortable."

"It doesn't seem to bother him." Hilt shrugged. "I'm not sure why that is. Cold, heat, brambles, whatever, he goes on wearing what he wears. I've often wondered how he does it. The other elves I've met aren't like that. Just Yntri and the other ancient ones that tend the Jharro grove."

"I see," Actually she didn't quite see. It was strange. She had been through so much, she had felt she'd seen it all, but Beth was realizing that there was a lot she hadn't seen. "So if he's taking the first watch, who is taking the second?"

"There's no need. He'll be taking all the watches. Yntri rarely sleeps. He tells me that it's because as you get older, you don't need as much sleep." The elf clicked from his perch up in the trees and Hilt nodded in amusement. "He adds that by the time you get to two thousand years old, sleep is a sign of laziness."

"Two thousand?" she looked up into the tree but all she could see was the end of the sapling shaking. That elf had a weird sense of humor.

They each found a place to bed down. Beth chose a flat piece of ground near the base of the rock that was free from pebbles and pine needles. Hilt chose a spot to her left, not far away. He sat next to the rock and pulled his knees up close, wrapping his coat around his legs as best he could and resting his head on his arms.

The ground was hard and her side ached, but the gauzy

blanket was so efficient at keeping out the cold that she felt almost cozy. She looked over at Hilt and his position looked so uncomfortable she felt guilty. After all, if she wasn't around, he would be the one using the blanket. She tried to push the guilt away, but it continued to gnaw at her.

"Come here, Hilt." Beth said finally.

"Hmm?" He turned a bleary eye her way.

"Come here. This blanket is big enough for both of us to share."

"I don't think that would be proper," he said.

Yntri snickered from somewhere in one of the trees above them.

"Shut up, Yntri," Beth said. "Hilt, we are both fully clothed and I trust that you will be a gentleman. Come here. I can see that you're cold."

Hilt crawled over and sat next to her, a hesitant look on his face. "How do you really know you can trust me? I'm a noble, after all. For all you know, I could be quite the ladies man."

She glanced at him. "Are you?"

"No," he said.

"That's good enough for me, now get under the blanket."

Hilt looked at her thoughtfully for a moment, then removed his overcoat, folded it twice lengthwise, and laid it down so both of them could rest their heads on it. Beth was grateful. That was much more comfortable then resting her head on the ground. He then laid down and scooted under the blanket. It ended up that though the elven blanket was indeed big enough to cover both of them, they had to scoot right up against each other to fit.

"Your sword is digging into my hip," Beth complained.

"Sorry."

"Do you always sleep with your sword belt on?"

"When I'm sleeping out in the wilderness I do," Hilt explained. "If something was to attack, I need to be ready."

"How can you sleep like that?" she wondered. "What if you

want to turn on your side?"

"I always sleep on my back. When I was young, my father taught me that if you sleep on your side, it's easier for something to sneak up on you."

"Well can you make an exception this one night? I have a bruise right there and the crossbar on your hilt is poking it."

"I suppose." He stood and removed the belt, then laid back next to her.

Beth was exhausted and though she should have fallen right to sleep, her mind was too active. She kept thinking about how long it had been since she had slept next to a man. She couldn't stop noticing the warmth from where their shoulders and hips were touching. It felt . . . nice. She frowned at herself. She needed to distract her mind.

"Hilt," she said, her tone sounding sharper than she intended. It wasn't his fault, after all. "You still haven't told me why you feel it is your duty to help me."

"Oh, well I suppose I haven't, have I?" He yawned. "I was almost asleep, you know."

"You can sleep after you tell me."

Hilt chuckled in response. It was such a warm sound that she found herself resisting the urge to snuggle up against him. She frowned again.

"Odd how it seems like every time I start to tell you, I'm interrupted." She could almost hear Hilt smiling as he said it.

"Just tell me before something else happens," Beth snapped, half expecting a troll to come running through the trees.

Hilt chuckled again. "Want to know what they never tell you about being named?"

"What's that?" Beth asked.

"Being named really isn't about how good you are."

"No?"

"Oh, in a way it is, I suppose, but the secret is that it's just another job. You become named and along with it comes a heap of responsibilities. People begin to expect things of you, especially the Prophet. He thrusts you into situations all the time. It's like he's the boss."

"So you decided to help me because it was part of your job?" she asked, a little disappointed.

"No. I knew that since he sent you across my path, he expected me to help. But it's more than that. I decided to help because, if the Prophet told you to climb this mountain, I knew it was the right thing to do." He paused. "That didn't sound fake, did it? Because I'm not being fake, I'm just being honest."

Now she wanted to hug him. What was wrong with her? "But how does it work? When you get named, do you sign an agreement? Does the Prophet meet with you and lay down the rules?"

"No," Hilt said. "I've met him from time to time but its not like that. He might show up and ask me to do something, but he never really tells me to do anything. Most of the time situations just fall in my lap and I know I'm supposed to deal with it."

"And it's the same way for other named warriors?"

"It seems to be, yes," He said with a shrug. "When, I see one, we tend to gripe about it together."

"That doesn't seem like a very good system," she said with a slight shake of her head. "What if the named warriors just decided not to do what he wanted? You didn't make any promises."

"But I don't think that would happen," Hilt said. "I could be wrong, but when I stood before the bowl, I could feel it searching my soul. It knew me. There is a lot of conjecture out there about what the bowl is looking for, and one of the key requirements is that you must know and trust in yourself. But more than that, I believe that one of the requirements is being someone that would make the right choice when asked. As far as an agreement . . ."

He slid his right hand under hers. "Feel that?"

She ran her fingers down the back of his hand. She could

feel the outline of his naming rune and the skin that it covered felt different, more leathery somehow. "Yes."

"That rune means a lot of things. It is an identification. It ties us to our naming weapons. It is a key that gets us into places other people would not be allowed to go. It's protection. It cannot be damaged, it cannot be removed." He withdrew his hand and continued, "Over the years I have come to realize that the naming rune is a symbol of a promise made not by our minds, but by our souls. Believe me I have railed against it with my mind multiple times, but in the end I could no more refuse to help than I could tell my heart to stop beating."

"Okay, I understand. You can go to sleep now," Beth said. Hilt chuckled, shaking his head at her oddity, but said no more. He fell asleep almost instantly.

She lay awake for a while longer, her hands clenched at her sides, her heart thumping. She had no excuse to feel this way. Hilt wasn't Coulton. She forced herself to breathe slowly and concentrated on the exhaustion she felt. Slowly, she drifted off to sleep.

Half way through the night, she was snuggled up against him.

VI

"Beth . . ." Hilt whispered. "Beth!"

"Hmm?" she said, snuggling closer.

"Um, my arm is asleep. Would you mind?"

She realized that she was laying on her side, one arm and leg wrapped around him and her head was resting on his arm. She lifted her head and squinted at him, noticing that she had drooled all over his shoulder. He had to have noticed, but at least he was kind enough not to mention it. She moved her leg and arm off of him and sat up. The sky was blue and brightening. It was morning.

She gave him a suspicious look. "How long have you been awake?"

"Not long," Hilt said, wincing as he massaged his tingling arm. "But you were snoring so peacefully, I hesitated to wake you."

"No, was I really?" He chuckled and she put her face in her hands. How humiliating. Coulton had never complained about her snoring, but Old Bob used to tease her about it. "Oh, I am so sorry."

"Not at all," Hilt said a grin. He stood and began folding the blanket. "I slept quite well actually once you stopped asking me for stories. The night was . . . quite comfortable."

Beth frowned trying to gauge his meaning. She watched him place the blanket back into his pack and put his swordbelt back on before she gave up. What did it matter? They would reach the peak that day and then Hilt could part ways with her. There was no reason to dwell on her actions during the night. The situation would not repeat itself. For some reason the thought made her sad.

A whistle echoed from beyond the camp and Yntri Yni entered with a bowl full of small greenish berries and four bulbous pieces of root.

"Is that breakfast you have, Yntri? Thank you!" Hilt said he glanced at Beth. "See, I told you Yntri was the perfect travel companion."

"What is it?" Beth asked as the elf held the bowl out to her.

"Frost berries and winnow root," Hilt said, popping a few berries into his mouth. "They aren't very flavorful, but not bad. These are two of the staples a traveler can scavenge for in higher altitudes like this. I am actually quite impressed that Yntri knows about them since this is such a different environment than the land he is from."

Yntri spoke at Hilt for several moments, his voice clicking with irritation and the warrior nodded, looking quite embarrassed. "I'm sorry, Yntri. I will try not to let that happen again."

"What was that about?" Beth asked.

"Uh, since we have been traveling with you, I have gotten into the habit of talking about him instead of to him. He was just reminding me that he is standing right here." Hilt gave Yntri an apologetic smile. "But seriously, Beth. Try the food. We have a ways yet to go today."

Beth tried the berries. Hilt was right. They were only vaguely sweet, but edible. The warrior took one of the roots and peeled back the rough outer skin with his knife. The skin came off quite easily in long strips and Hilt gave her one. It had a clean crisp taste and a consistency very much like an apple.

"This is quite good, Yntri. Thank you," she said.

The elf nodded and bit into one of the roots himself. He didn't bother peeling it. While he munched on it, he walked over and climbed the tree he had stayed in during the night. For the first time, Beth noticed a large pile of wood shavings at the base of the tree. What had the elf been up to?

A few moments later, the elf slid back down the trunk. Beth

winced, knowing what such a slide would have done to her bare feet. In one hand, Yntri held a small wooden bowl and in the other, he carried a bow. He had a wide grin on his ancient face, and he gestured to her, smiling as he clicked at her.

"Beth, this bow is for you." Hilt said in surprise. He gave her an impressed look. "This is amazing. Yntri is one of the greatest weapon makers alive. He has made weapons exclusively for the Roo-tan for centuries, so to make this for you is the rarest of exceptions."

Beth looked at the bow more closely as the elf approached. The wood was stained a dark ebony and the handle was wrapped with viper skin. Tiny runic symbols had been carved along its length but they weren't symbols she recognized. She was pretty sure they weren't elemental runes at all. Perhaps they were words in Yntri's language.

The importance of this gift settled upon her. Beth could not think of a proper way to respond, so she did something she hadn't done since she was a child. She gave the elf a deep curtsey. "Thank you, Yntri. I-I don't know what to say. I am honored, but . . . but why would you make this for me? What did I do to deserve this?"

Yntri gave her a kind smile and clicked his response. "Yntri says that when he listened to your heart, your spirit cried out to him. It has been a long time since he has crafted a weapon that wasn't made from Jharro wood. But the Jharro Grove only gives weapons to its protectors and he knew he had to make you this bow."

Beth reached for the bow. "I will cherish it always. Thank-."

Yntri pulled the bow back and waggled a finger. "He says that there is something you must do before you can wield the bow."

"The sapling he found was strong and lively. It shaped itself to him willingly, but the viper gave conditions, he . . ." Hilt frowned. "I am not quite sure how to translate this. Yntri, would you repeat that last part?"

The elf clicked some more, motioning at the bow while he

talked and Hilt looked quite perplexed at first, but finally he nodded. "He says that he took the soul of the viper you killed and bound it to the bow."

"The soul of the viper?" Beth said. She shifted to mage sight and looked at the bow. She saw nothing. No magical elements at all. "How could he do that?"

Yntri explained. "He says that he is a soul taster and a shaper. It is how he makes the weapon to fit the wielder. He inserted the viper's fangs into the handle, then combined the fat, brains, and venom of the viper and used it to polish the wood. He then wrapped the handle with the viper's skin and coated the bow with sap from the Jharro tree so that it would cure quickly and bind the viper's soul to the bow.

"He says that you were the one that killed the viper and that you consumed its flesh, so he already had a link to work with. But the . . ." Hilt scratched his head and he sounded a bit unsure when he continued, "The viper is . . . perturbed at you. He says it was upset that you did not fight it fairly. He explained to it that this was how a human defeats a viper, but it is insistent. The viper will only bend its will to yours if you let it bite you first."

"What?" Beth said in both confusion and alarm.

Yntri shook his head and clicked some more.

"Oh," Hilt said. "Sorry, I was a bit off with that last part. He says that the viper will only bend its will to you if you taste its venom. Once you do that, the link will be complete."

Yntri lifted the small wooden bowl in his other hand and Beth saw that it contained a pink waxy paste.

"Is that the same stuff you polished the bow with?"

Yntri nodded.

"I don't want to taste that," Beth said. Snake brains and venom weren't something any sane person would eat. Besides, she had studied at the Mage School for several years and this just wasn't the way magic worked. "Really, why I would want a snake's soul bound to me, anyway?"

Yntri's eyes widened and he put a finger to his lips. "Yntri says that now is not the time to offend it," Hilt translated. "He says that even the smallest of souls are powerful things and that the soul of a viper is a very useful companion for an archer to have."

Beth winced. This was obviously important to Yntri, but the idea was still ridiculous. "Yntri, I do not want to offend you or the snake, but I looked at the bow with my mage sight and there is no magic in it. I-I respect your traditions, but do we really have to go through with this part?"

Yntri laughed then, long and hard. "He says that your Mage School has forgotten the old ways. He says that the power of the spirit can not be seen by your mage eyes. This is why the wizards don't understand his people's ways and also why they don't understand the Prophet's ways." The withered old elf's face grew serious then. He clicked out a very clear question. "He asks you to show him some of that same faith you showed the Prophet."

The request caught her off guard. He had a point. What reason did she have to doubt him? Beth pushed away her misgivings. "Okay Yntri. What do I need to do?"

The elf slung the new bow over one shoulder, then stood in front of her. He reached two fingers into the bowl and scooped out a glob of the pink waxy substance and clicked instructions.

Hilt stood at her side, offering calm assurance. "He says stand very still. He is going to place the venom of the viper on your lips. When he does, the snake will attack. Stand firm against it. Withstand its bite and bend it to your will. Then the bow will be yours."

"Is this going to hurt?"

She looked into the elf's ancient eyes and felt a sense of calm wash over her. This was a gift and Yntri was a friend. He would not hurt her. Besides, Hilt was by her side. Everything would be all right.

Yntri raised the two fingers to her face and she smelled nothing. He rubbed the paste across her lips, pushing some of it into her mouth. It tasted like mint, with just the slightest metallic aftertaste. Beth realized that she was tasting the sap of the Jharro tree. A warmth spread from her lips across her face and down her throat followed by numbness. Then came the burn. It started at her lips and tongue, then spread up her face and down her throat.

She closed her eyes and the visage of the viper rose before her. It hissed and struck, sinking its fangs into her lips. There was no pain, but she felt it pierce her flesh. She reached up, grasped the snake around the back of its head and squeezed, forcing its mouth open. She pulled it away from her face and glared at it. Its eyes met hers and she felt its acceptance.

When Beth opened her eyes, the world was blurry and bouncing back and forth around her. She couldn't feel her face. She could still feel the skin of the viper in her hand, but it was stiff and unyielding. Beth realized that she had the handle of the bow gripped in her fist.

She blinked a few times, and the world cleared somewhat. She was leaning forward, resting on something. She turned her head and looked right into Hilt's ear. Somehow she was hanging onto him, her arms wrapped loosely around his neck and he was hiking along, holding onto her legs, carrying her on his back.

"Hilt, put me downed," she said. Her lips were numb, but at least they still worked.

"Beth! You're awake!" he said.

"Put me down, Hilt!"

He crouched and let go of her legs so that she could stand. Once she had her feet under her, she pushed away from him and swung around looking for Yntri. The elf stood not far away, grinning at her. She would have stormed over to him if she had full control of her legs. Instead she stumbled towards him.

"You!" Beth didn't know what she was going to do when she reached the elf. She felt like throwing a punch at him, but she was so woozy she was pretty sure she'd miss. Perhaps just throttling him would be better. But when she stood in front of him, she couldn't do it. "If you weren't two thousand years old, I'd punch that grin off your face."

Yntri just clicked pleasantly at her and held out a quiver made of wood and squirrel fur. She ignored the offering.

"You didn't prepare me for that! First thing when I wake up in the morning you say, 'Here, eat this snake venom?' You should give a woman some time to get her wits about her before you ask her to make important decisions. And you!" She said, swinging her arm around to point at Hilt. "I can't believe you helped him talk me into it. 'Oh, Beth, this is so amazing. He is one of the greatest weapon makers ever!' You are supposed to be on my side!"

Hilt watched her tirade with an amused expression on his face. "I told Yntri that you would not be happy when you woke up." She started towards him with a fist pulled back and he raised both hands defensively. "I promise I didn't know that was going to happen. When you passed out, I very nearly punched him myself."

Yntri grabbed her arm, halting her progress, and twirled her around to face him. He was strong for a wrinkled old elf. He held out the quiver and clicked insistently.

"Let go of me."

"He's asking you to shoot an arrow first. If you are still angry, then you are welcome to punch him . . . and kick him." Hilt said. "I added that last part, by the way."

She reached for the quiver, but stopped herself. "Is this magic too? I am not eating squirrel brains so that it can bite my spirit. I am telling you that right now."

"That should not be necessary. I saw him put it together as we walked and I don't think it is magical at all." Hilt said, then paused and looked at the elf. "Right Yntri?"

Yntri simply rolled his eyes and thrust the quiver into her hands.

Beth looked at it more closely. The quiver was made of two curved pieces of bark bound together with squirrel skin. The inside had been scraped smooth and held a dozen arrows. They looked to be freshly made. The wood was supple and smelled of pine.

"How did you find time to make these?" she asked.

Yntri shrugged and clicked a response. "He's had a lot of experience," Hilt explained. "He carries arrowheads and feathers in his pack to make more as he needs them along the way."

Beth slung the quiver over one shoulder and drew an arrow. She realized that she was still gripping the bow. It felt good to hold a bow again. The viper skin grip was comfortable and formed perfectly to match her hand. She had to admit the elf knew his craft. She looked around for a target to aim for and froze.

"Where the hell are we?" she said in confusion.

They stood on a ridgeline with a steep drop off on either side. The peak seemed much closer, yet there were many trees nearby and at the bottom of the slope to her left was a large and placid lake. The area below was lush and green, very different from any other part of the mountain she had seen.

"Quite stunning isn't it?" Hilt said, walking up beside her. "Yntri says that this is a place of new life. Just a few years ago it was a barren mountainside. Now life springs up all around it."

"How can he tell that?" she asked.

"Most of the trees down around the lake are new, maybe five years old. The rest of the greenery is grass and flowers."

"You were down there?" Beth asked incredulously.

"Passed it on the way up here," Hilt said. "I was hoping we might be able to fish, but Yntri said there weren't any yet."

"That's a long way down. How long was I out?" she asked.

"Nearly two hours," Hilt replied.

"And you carried me all this way?"

"I promised to get you to the top, didn't I?" Hilt said with a grin. "Believe me, I had to keep reminding my legs that. My body isn't what it used to be."

She gave him a curt nod. "Very well, you're forgiven." Beth leaned in and surprised him with a kiss on the cheek. She then speared Yntri with a steely glare. "We'll see about you."

Beth lifted the bow again and sighted a lightning split tree fifty feet away. As she drew the arrow back to her ear, she could feel the viper coil, ready to strike. The world around her blurred and there was only the target. She released the shot and as the arrow neared her target, her mind's eye saw not the arrow, but the viper, its mouth opened, fangs bared. The arrow struck with a sharp crack.

They walked over to the tree.

"You hit the trunk," Hilt said with an impressed smile. "Not bad for someone who hasn't lifted a bow in years."

"I wasn't aiming for the trunk. I was aiming for that knot," She said pointing to the dark twisted spot where her arrow stuck. When she pulled out the arrow, she noticed a latticework of cracks extending from the strike point. While Hilt examined the knot, Beth walked back to Yntri. The elf gave her an appreciative nod.

"Yntri, I forgive you." She bent and kissed his wrinkled forehead. "This is a fine gift." The elf turned his head and pointed at his cheek and she kissed that too. He smiled and pointed to his other cheek. Beth snorted. "Don't get carried away."

She slung the bow over her shoulder and when she let go, felt a twinge of pain in her forearm. Her hand was clenched and it hurt to spread her fingers open.

"Ow," she said, rubbing her cramped muscles. "Was I holding this bow the whole time?"

"Like you wanted to choke it," Hilt said. "I wantedhilts to take it from you but Yntri said not to try."

Yntri whistled to get their attention, then clicked at them, motioning to them that it was time to move along. The elf started off, not bothering to check if they had followed.

They hiked along the top of the ridgeline, heading towards the peak. The mountains rise had been fairly gradual before, but she could see sharp inclines and cliffs ahead. It would make for a strenuous day, but she wasn't worried about the climb. There would be a way and they would make it, she was sure. The thing that made Beth's heart tighten was the thought that the end was near. What would happen once she stood there?

The ridge ended in a rocky spire that they weren't equipped to climb. They had to edge around it and climb down the slope a ways to find a better way up. Yntri was as surefooted and nimble as any young elf, and Hilt was confident and deliberate in his movements, but Beth had never attempted such precarious climbs before and Hilt had to reach out and steady her several times.

It looked as though they were going to have to backtrack, wasting several hours of daylight, when Yntri spotted the waterfall. The mountain stream that poured down from the cliff above had carved down into the rock, leaving a series of landings that looked quite climbable. The only downside was the stiff fall breeze that blew. Already, the mist blown from the falling water had struck Beth with an icy chill.

In the end, they had no choice. There was no guarantee that they would find a better place to climb elsewhere. They stepped into the waters flow and found to their relief that the water was not as cold as they had feared. Evidently it fed from a hot spring somewhere above. Yntri started up the short cliff face towards the first landing, making it look easy. Beth was to follow right behind him with Hilt taking up the rear so that he could help her if she got stuck.

Beth watched as Yntri disappeared over the first ledge. The elf stuck his head back over and motioned her up, but she stood frozen. She glanced at Hilt. "How am I supposed to climb with a river falling in my face?"

"That's not a river. That's barely a trickle. Here," Hilt pulled the coil of rope out of his bag and tied one end around his waist, then tied the other end around hers. "Now you know that if you fall, I will be able to catch you."

Beth's nose wrinkled. "What are you talking about? I am a grown woman. If I fall, I'll just end up jerking you down with me."

"Then consider it a show of my faith that you can do this." Hilt said with a grin.

Beth nodded and reached for the first hand hold, then turned back. "And what if you fall?"

"Then at least we die together. Now go already."

The first stretch of the climb actually wasn't too difficult. Hand holds and foot holds were plentiful and there was a slight slope to the cliff face. The only problem was that the warmth of the water allowed lichen and moss to grow in abundance which made for some slippery holds. They reached the half way mark without any difficulties and Beth was gaining confidence in her climbing abilities.

The next stretch was the toughest. The cliff face was sheer and high and covered with a blanket of red lichen. The falling water was fanned out evenly across the entire surface, making it treacherously slippery. They changed their strategy for this climb. Yntri would go first, followed by Hilt. Then the two of them would stand at the top and hold the rope to anchor her just in case she slipped.

Yntri started up with Hilt close behind, following the elf's every movement carefully. The lichen was so thick in places that they had to dig through it to get to hand holds. At one point, Yntri was in lichen up to his elbows. Then it seemed as if the entire cliff face moved. The wall of lichen slid over Yntri, obscuring him from view.

There was a cry of pain and a series of panicked clicks and whistles. The wall of lichen rippled and shifted, then pieces started flying away. Yntri's form re-emerged, but the lichen swarmed back over him as if attacking. The elf clung to the rock with one hand while the other whipped about with his bow, knocking chunks of lichen through the air. A few pieces fell at her feet.

Beth's hand flew to her mouth as she realized that this wasn't lichen at all. Tiny legs sprouted from the base of its leaf-like body and clawed at the air trying to find purchase. As soon as it righted itself, the creature promptly crawled back up the cliff face. She looked back up and saw Hilt become enveloped by the shifting mass. A series of shouts and curses erupted from his position.

"Those are lichen spiders!" Beth shouted. They were fairly common in the tinny woods. "Don't worry, they leave a nasty bite but they're not poisonous! You must have climbed into a nest!"

"You think?" shouted Hilt between swears.

"Just keep climbing!" she yelled. "And don't fall!"

The two men struggled the rest of the way up the cliff face, shouting and grunting, but both made it to the top safely. After a few minutes knocking the spiders off of their bodies they threw down the rope. Beth tied the rope around her waist and took a deep breath to calm her nerves.

"Sorry, Beth. We'll pull you up as quickly as we can!" She could hear Yntri clicking and Hilt yelled back down! "Don't be scared. It's really not that bad!"

"They're just spiders!" Beth shouted back up at them and started to climb.

She only made it up a few steps before the rope was yanked up under her arms and she was pulled away from her hand holds. The stupid men were trying to be helpful, hoisting her up as promised, but it really hurt. She wanted to shout up at them to stop, but could only hiss as the rope dug into the bruises from the day before. She dangled helplessly, letting out a series of pained gasps as she rose. To make things worse, the wind blew against her wet dress, chilling her to the bone.

The rope began to sway back and forth. She swung gently at first, then in wider and wider arcs, aided by the rhythm of their pulling. She bumped into the cliff face once, swung away, then slammed into it over and over again as they pulled, sending spiders flying through the air. The swinging steadied as she neared the top, but by the time they grabbed her arms and dragged her over the edge, she felt positively battered.

When they pulled her to the top, Beth sat down with a splash. The water was much warmer up there. She rolled to her back, letting the water run over her, soothing her battered body. She let out a groan.

"Beth, are you okay?" Hilt asked in concern.

"No! That really hurt! " Beth snapped. "I don't think there is a single part of me that isn't bruised right now!"

"Sorry," Hilt winced. "We were trying to get you past the spiders as quickly as we could."

"I would so hit you if I felt like moving right now," she

growled.

"How many times did they bite you?" he asked.

"None. Though you probably smashed a hundred of them with my body," Beth said. With great effort, she sat up and rolled to her knees. She held her hand out to Hilt. "Well? Help me up."

"How did you not get bit?" Hilt asked as he pulled Beth to her feet. He drew back his jacket sleeve to show a series of angry red marks along his forearm. "Yntri and I are covered in welts."

"They're spiders," she said as if it was obvious. She gazed up at the last stretch of cliff ahead of them. It looked quite mild in comparison to the rest of the climb. "Creatures don't attack me. I've told you before."

"But they quelled you. How would that still work?" Hilt said.

Beth shrugged. "I don't know. Believe me, I've asked myself that same question countless times. Maybe they missed some piece of my magic. Maybe it was deep down inside me in a place they couldn't touch. I don't know. I can't control it. All I know is it's the last piece of magic I have left and I can't even see it with my mage sight. Who knows? Maybe it's the way I smell."

"I doubt it." Hilt chuckled. "I mean, we could all use a good bathing, but it didn't work for Yntri or I."

"That's not what I meant, idiot," she said with a glower. "But thanks for pointing that out."

"Oh come on." Hilt said. "I said we."

"I know what you meant," she said and walked to the wall in front of her. "Besides, your excuse doesn't work. We both know that Yntri just smells like almonds."

Beth started up the final stretch of the climb in the lead. Yntri chuckled and clicked at Hilt.

"Yeah, yeah. I know," he grumbled and took up the rear.

Once at the top of the cliff, the stream, circled around to their left. The water was so warm that it steamed in the cold air, surrounding the area in a thick mist. They followed the stream for a short distance, but they couldn't make out their surroundings so they walked away from the water and stood at the edge of a rocky ledge hoping that the mist would disperse enough that they could get their bearings.

The didn't have to wait long before the wind changed and blew the mist away from them, revealing their goal. They could see the highest peak clearly now, standing across the ridge ahead of them. It was surrounded by a sheer cliff a hundred feet high.

"No, not another cliff," Hilt complained. "I have had enough climbing to last a lifetime."

"No whining," Beth reprimanded, gazing at the mountaintop. "We are almost there."

"Are you sure we'll even be able to climb that once we get there?" Hilt said. "That cliff looks pretty steep."

"There will be a way. I know it," she said with confidence. "The Prophet would not send us this far if there wasn't a way to reach the top."

The frustration on Hilt's face melted away and he sighed. "You are right, Beth. This is just the last stretch."

An excited series of clicks and whistles rang out from the mist. Hilt looked at Beth and shrugged. "He's found the source of the stream and wants us to come see."

They headed back into the mist and could hear the gush of the water before they saw it. Yntri appeared before them and grabbed their hands, a wide grin on his ancient face. He pulled them along the water's edge until they saw it. Beth and Hilt stopped and stared.

Rising out of the mist was a great boulder at least twice Hilt's height. A human hand print was impressed into the rock about a third of the way up. A large hole opened at the base of the palm and hot water gushed out.

"What is this?" Beth asked.

In response, Yntri trotted up to the boulder and ran his fingers over the hand print in the rock. All the while, clicking at them.

"He says that this is the source," Hilt translated. "This is the water that carved out our path in the cliff face. This is the spring that feeds the lake below."

"I see that. And it is strange that there is a hand print there, but what does that mean to us?" Beth asked.

Yntri sat on the ground cross legged next to the boulder and placed his Jharro bow across his lap. He took a small tin out of his pack and opened it to reveal a white paste. He clicked at Hilt for a moment, then closed his eyes and began to sing. It was a low intonation interspersed with clicks. While he sang, Yntri dipped his fingers into the paste and began rubbing it into his skin.

"What is he doing?" Beth asked.

"He is preparing himself," Hilt said, his brow knit in concern.

"Preparing for what?" Beth asked, a sudden ominous chill running up her spine.

"He says we are nearing a holy place. He is preparing for battle."

VII

"What does he mean when he says we are nearing a holy place?" Beth asked. "And why does that mean a battle?"

She turned to see Hilt's concern turn into a smile.

"That means holy guardians," he said, gripping his sword hilts with both hands. "Whenever there is a holy place where men are not allowed, guardians are placed."

Beth swallowed. "What are these guardians like?"

"Misshapen beasts. Immortal hungry creatures whose only reason for existence is to devour those that come too close," he said, nearly giggling with excitement.

Beth put her face in her hands. She had seen that expression on his face before, right before he blundered into the cave looking for the behemoth. "And I take it these holy guardians are one of these creatures of legend you are so eager to fight."

"No, but they are the next best thing. No one makes it past the guardians." Hilt noticed her expression and frowned. "Don't look at me like that, Beth. I didn't come here seeking them out."

"Yes, but if they are holy guardians, why would we want to find them?" she asked. "Let's just leave them alone and get to the top of this mountain."

Hilt looked at her in disbelief. "Don't you see? The top of the mountain is exactly the place they will be guarding. It has to be. Look, Yntri knows it."

The elf continued to rock back and forth, singing his little chant. He had covered two thirds of his body with the white paste and the tin was nearly empty. Beth shook her head.

"But why would the Prophet send me to the top of the mountain if no one is allowed up there?" It made no sense. Surely if he meant for her to arrive he would open the way.

"That's why he sent you to me," Hilt said, his smile sure and confident. "I am here to help you fight your way to the top. Yntri was here to make you a bow. The Prophet planned it this way."

Beth wanted to smack the smile off his face. It was that stupid pride of his again. Still, she couldn't refute his logic. Everything had indeed fallen into place to set up this moment. "Just promise me that we won't fight these guardians unless it is absolutely necessary."

"Of course," Hilt said as if it was ridiculous of her to think he would do so. "You don't seek out a fight with holy guardians unless you're on the wrong side. You only fight them if you have to."

A frightening thought came to her. What if this really was what the Prophet had intended. She went into the forest seeking death. What if he had sent her to die up here instead? What if her whole purpose in coming was to drag these two men along? Hilt, handsome, honorable, and reckless; Yntri, ancient and wise. What if they were all supposed to die up here to fulfill some strange purpose?

Yntri finished his chanting and stood. He was covered in white from head to toe, his ancient brown eyes the only bit of color. He clicked at them and began to walk.

As they started up the ridgeline towards the cliffs ahead, Beth felt sick with worry. And she was angry with the attitudes of her companions. It wasn't just about Hilt. Yntri looked so happy. What was wrong with these men?

"I don't understand, Yntri," she said. "I expect Hilt to be crazy, but why are you so pleased to go into this battle?"

Yntri clicked a response and Hilt said, "He has felt the weight of importance about your journey from the beginning. But he made a realization last night as you told your tale. For some reason, he feels like the end to his centuries of searching is tied to you."

Was it as she feared? Beth swallowed. "But why? What is he searching for?"

"I don't know," Hilt says. "I've known him for years and he has never told me."

"Yntri," Beth said with pleading tone. "Tell me. What are you searching for on these pilgrimage of yours?"

The elf clicked an answer.

"He searches for the true seeds," Hilt translated. He frowned. "Yntri, neither of us knows what that means."

The elf gave him a pensive look, then directed his gaze to Beth. He moved up beside her and held out his hand. It was covered in the same white paste that covered the rest of his body. She glanced at Hilt, but the warrior just shrugged. Yntri gave an encouraging nod and she held his hand and they continued up the sloping ridgeline.

A strange warmth emanated from Yntri's hand. Beth felt it enter her skin. The warmth was familiar and she recognized it as the sap from the Jharro tree. She had felt it when Yntri smeared the venom on her lips. The warmth traveled up her arm and neck, settling between her eyes. Her vision began to drift and Yntri began to talk. As Hilt translated, a vision formed in her mind.

Yntri's earliest memory was of standing at his mothers' knee and watching his father converse with a human man. The man came and knelt in front of him and reached out. Yntri toddled into the man's arms and was lifted up. The man smiled and spoke with him and though Yntri could not remember the man's face, he remembered feeling safe in the man's arms.

Yntri's parents followed as the man took him through the Jharro grove and came upon a tree. This one was young and unruly, only fifty feet high. So far it had rejected the hands of his people as young Jharro were oft to do. But as the man reached out and touched the warm gray wood of the tree, its trunk split open. The man kissed Yntri on the forehead and placed him inside. The tree accepted him within and closed around him, encasing him in sap. He learned of the young tree and it learned of him. When he was born again from its trunk, his parents were waiting for him but the human man was gone.

This man, whom Yntri came to know as the Prophet returned to the Jharro grove every hundred years or so. He would speak with Yntri's people and initiate the young ones. Eventually Yntri sired his own child and the Prophet came to speak with him. He told Yntri of the importance of maintaining the grove and of passing on the knowledge of the old ways and Yntri covenanted to do just that.

The wilderness around the Jharro grove eventually grew wild and untamed. His people maintained the grove and kept it clear of weeds and unclean creatures and kept to themselves. But men and monsters learned of the magic of the Jharro tree and came seeking its power. Yntri was put in charge of protecting the trees from encroachers, and there were many wars and many deaths.

When the Prophet next returned, he was saddened. The grove had been damaged, with many of the trees dead or dying and Yntri's people had dwindled to a fraction of their number.

The Prophet soon guided a large tribe of humans to the grove. They were the Roo, an uncultured but proud people that had been driven from their land. The Prophet brokered an arrangement between their people and Yntri's. The Roo could settle in the land around the grove and Yntri's people would teach them and provide them weapons from the Jharro trees. In exchange, the Roo would protect the Jharro grove. The Roo-Tan nation was born.

The Jharro grove grew again for a time, but slowly. Then it stopped growing all together. The trees stopped producing seeds and one day nearly two hundred years ago, the Prophet had returned again. This time he met with Yntri and gave him a mission. Sensing that the grove was in danger, the Prophet had traveled the known lands and planted Jharro trees in obscure places. Once a year, Yntri was to leave the grove and travel to one of these locations to try and harvest seeds from these trees. These new seeds would have new life and new memories that would revive and replenish the grove.

Yntri had accepted the mission with excitement, but he had not known how frustrating these pilgrimages were going to be. Successful trips were few and far between. Sometimes the trees had been discovered and cut down, but more often the tree he found had grown wild and strange. The few times he had found thriving trees, he had left them with trepidation knowing that they were vulnerable without a caretaker and also knowing that his people were too few in number to look after the trees themselves.

It had been fifty years since he had last found a viable tree and most of the grove had grown stale and stagnant. A few of the oldest trees, including his father's and mother's trees had become stiff and unmaleable, refusing to talk to the elves at all. Yntri feared that the days of the Jharro tree were coming to an end.

This year he had ended his pilgrimage despondent. The tree he found had become foul and rotten, inhabited by an evil thing. But he had met two humans with strong spirits, heirs of the bow. One he had left to ripen on his own, but Beth was nearly ready. The time for his mission to end was fast approaching.

Beth took a deep breath and realized that Yntri had released her hand. Her mind slowly returned to the present. Hilt was standing beside her, speaking to the elf in hushed tones. He had his swords drawn and ready.

They had arrived. She stood at the top of the ridgeline and saw the cliff that protected the peak rising before her. She looked back at the long ridgeline behind them. How had she missed the climb?

"What do you want to do, Beth?" Hilt asked. "The cliff is too sheer, but maybe there is a way farther down or around the other side."

"Yntri . . . his story . . ." The elf watched the path before them. He was ancient and small, but such a heavy responsibility rested on his shoulders.

"I know," Hilt said, his kind eyes taking in her confused

gaze with concern. "And I hope that he finds his answer here just as surely as I know you will. Now, focus with me. This is your quest. Are you ready to proceed?"

Beth turned her attention to the path ahead. This place was strange. Hilt was right about the cliff wall. It was unnaturally smooth and unmarred. There would be no hand holds. At least none that she would be able to use. At the bottom of the cliff was a wide flat area clustered with trees. But they weren't pines like she would expect, but lush leafy trees, as green as if it were summer.

"I think you're right. We need to continue along the side of the cliff and find a way up," she said and realized how obvious the statement was. It was the only option they had. Hilt had only asked her the question to help her clear her mind. She looked along the cliff base and saw round shadows periodically through the trees. "What are those round shadows, just at the cliffs base?"

"Caves, we think," Hilt said and now that her focus had returned, he was once again brimming with excitement. "Maybe that's where the guardians live. Or maybe there is a way to climb to the top from within the mountain. We won't know until we scout it out."

Beth nodded and pulled her bow from her back. The viper awakened at her touch. She drew an arrow. "Let's go."

They walked down to the base of the cliff and Beth realized something else strange. Her clothes were still damp from their climb up the waterfall, but she didn't feel a chill. She hadn't since Yntri had started his story. The air here should have been frigid, but it was warm as a spring day.

When they reached the tree line, they found a pathway stretching along the cliffs base. It was clean and free of leaves as if it had been well maintained. They stood in front of it and looked hesitantly at one another until Hilt stepped boldly onto the pathway.

Beth felt a strange stirring inside her. There was a slight ringing in her ears and her vision tightened around the edges. Shadows moved within the trees. Whispers rang out in her ears. No. The whispers were in her mind. She couldn't make them out at first, but then they became louder, more insistent, a chorus of voices, each one unique. Each one plaintive.

"*Named one*." "*Leave*." "*So hungry*." "*Ancient one*." "*Come*." "*Eat you*."

Beth looked at Hilt and Yntri. They were looking at her with the same question. Hilt pointed to his head and nodded. She felt a slight sense of relief that they heard the voices too.

"*LEAVE THIS PLACE*." "*Dance with meeee*." "*Your answer . . .*" "*Play with us*." "*EAT YOU!*" "*Witch*."

"Witch?" Beth said, gritting her teeth. She tightened her grip on her bow. "What do we do?"

"*Run*." "*Come*." "*So tasty*." "*LEAVE*."

"We have no choice," Hilt said and Yntri nodded. "We fight. It's the only way to reach the top."

"*Devour*!" "*BONES*." "*Come, witch*."

"But the voices . . ." Beth said, resisting the urge to place her hands over her ears.

"It's part of their attack," Hilt said. His body was at the same time loose and ready, yet tensed like a coiled spring. "They're trying to scare us, distract us, drive us mad. You need to ignore them."

"*Named one*." "*Eat*." "*Eat!*" "*Witch*." "*EAT YOU ALL*!"

Beth looked to Yntri. The white paste on his skin glowed eerily and he nodded at her. She looked back to Hilt. "I'm ready."

"Good. Stay between us and shoot when you have an opening," he said, and they started down the path.

"*YES!*" "*Yesss*." "*EAT YOU!!*"

Shadows moved all around them. Yntri released an arrow into the trees. Hilt swung his blades, sending blades of air ahead of them. Crashes resounded, roars erupted, and the voices exulted.

"*The pain*!" "*Ancient one*!" "*Yes*!"

Beth pulled an arrow back and whipped around with her bow, searching for a target. The viper hissed in anticipation, ready to spring, but she could not see anything more than vague shapes among the trees. She shifted to mage sight.

She saw them now. The guardians were mutated irregular beasts. Their anatomy seemed to make no sense. Some had the head of a dog, others birds. Some had multiple heads, extra arms. Some were hairy or scaled or feathered. The only thing they had in common were mouths, gaping toothy mouths in their chests.

"*Come.*" "*Come.*" "*Hungry . . .*" "*Witch.*"

"Stop calling me witch!" She released her arrow at a guardian with the head of a three-eyed cat. The viper struck the middle eye with pleasure. It fell to the ground, shuddering.

Yntri cried out and she saw a large beast with yellow scales hurtle off of the mountain edge, speared by his arrow. Another beast rose in front of her, but great golden blades of air cut it in two and continued into the trees, shearing off branches as they went.

"*Blood!*" "*EAT YOU!*"

Beth gathered her courage and fired again and again. Each arrow striking with the viper's bite, knocking the beasts to the ground convulsing and foaming from their chest mouths. She was going to have to ask Yntri how it worked.

She stepped forward with confidence, felling guardians until she realized with a panic that she was out of arrows. She could hear Yntri and Hilt fighting to either side, but could not see them.

"Hilt!" she cried and a gigantic beast came out of the trees ahead. Its head was that of a spider with multiple round eyes, but it had the body of a serpent. It reared up in front of her and she knew that she wouldn't be able to run from its grasp.

But the guardian didn't attack. It slithered around her and headed towards the commotion Hilt was causing. Beth watched it go in confusion, then noticed other guardians flowing through the forest to either side of her. None of them came her way.

Why didn't they attack? Was it her power? How could it work against holy beasts like these when it didn't faze the trolls? Then it came to her. She was meant to be here. The Prophet told her to come. The guardians weren't there for her.

She turned and saw something through the trees ahead. A stairway. She put her bow over her shoulder and walked closer.

The stairs curved up the cliff face, each looking as if chiseled by hand. This was it. This was where the Prophet intended her to go. She could feel something above calling out to her. Beth approached the bottom step.

"*She comes.*" "*Hungry!*" "*Wait.*" "*She comes.*" "*Witch.*"

Hungry eyes and dark shapes watched her from the cave at the foot of the stair, but they did not approach. She climbed the stairs slowly, the yearning within her echoed by a yearning from the top of the mount. As she continued higher and higher, the voices of the guardians faded from her mind and instead she heard another, softer voice.

It started small, little more then a whisper. She had to strain to hear it. Then it grew steadily, increasing with each step. She couldn't understand the words, yet her mouth moved along with them. It was a joyous, welcoming sound. Beth felt something building up, swelling inside her. Words began to bubble forth from her lips; strange, prayer-like tones.

Beth felt a sudden weakness come over her. Darkness clouded her vision and it became a struggle to make each step. Her feet began to slide towards the stairs' edge. Something was pulling at her. Beth strained to keep her feet. She looked up. She could see the top. The end was so near!

She fell to her knees and crawled, a dark weight bearing her down. Her feet continued to be pulled to the edge. The thing within her swelled even more, growing until she thought she would burst. She was shouting now, strange words in an unfamiliar language. She was only a few steps away. One foot was dragged over the edge. She lunged towards the top step, touching it with her fingertips . . .

The pressure bearing down on her eased and the pulling stopped. Beth stumbled up over the last step and collapsed on a flat stone bench. She looked up and despite the daylight, she saw the stars. They were so very close. The swelling within her moved up past her lungs and through her throat, pouring into her head. She feared her skull would burst, but it didn't. Her mind opened up, drinking it all in.

The world unfolded before her eyes. Millions of tiny pinpricks of light dotted the lands before her, each one an individual's life. Somehow she knew that all she had to do was reach out and touch one of those lights to see the person's life laid out before her. But Beth had no need to search those people. She reached inside herself instead.

There was a blaze of light and she saw her life roll by before her. The joys, the sadness, the pleasure, the pain, reliving it all in an instant. She felt a sense of dread as her husband's death approached. Tears streaming down her face, she skipped forward to the present and saw herself laying on a stone altar surrounded by whispery runes.

She reminded herself why she was there. The Prophet had promised her answers. But what was the question? Had she ever decided?

"What now?" she whispered. She had been heading to her death when the Prophet redirected her. Perhaps that was her question. "Live or die?"

With a flash, her future paths spread out before her. It was like the vision she had seen in the fire, but much more clear and detailed. When she chose death each path was short and many of them quite painful. There were so many ways to die, but what then? What happened after death? The vision would not say.

If she chose to live, many other paths opened before her, some of them satisfying, some of them depressing, but the vision was fickle and left some other paths blurred. One thing was certain. In none of those futures was Coulton alive again. Perhaps death was the right option.

Her reverie was disturbed by sounds from below. There were shouts and roars. Crashes and cracks. A battle was approaching the stairs. A voice rang out from the ether. It was shouting her name.

"Hilt!" she gasped.

The vision zoomed Hilt's figure to the forefront of her mind. He was battling the guardians below, searching for her. She wished he would go away and leave her to her fate, but she knew Hilt's pride would not let him accept defeat. His future rolled before her and it was short. He was strong, but his enemy was limitless. He never made it to the top of the stairs. She watched him die multiple times at the guardian's hands, each time torn apart and devoured. There was only one path in which he had a future and that was if she came down and stopped him.

"But then what?" She grumbled. The vision followed his path further. His future spread out like a tree, each choice he made starting another branch. She followed all the possible directions his life could take. Most were very short, and almost all of them were violent. As she feared, he had grown impatient. She watched him die in battle countless times. Always for pride. She scowled. Hilt's pride. It would be his undoing.

"The idiot." He needed someone to temper him. At that suggestion, one path stood out, one path that startled her. This pathway steered him differently, leading to a new set of choices. This was the only pathway in which Hilt lived and in this path, there was only one constant that led him in the correct direction. In each of those crucial moments she was at his side.

"But why?" Why would she choose to stay with him? Hilt was a nobleman and a warrior, cocky, arrogant, and rash; traits she had never found appealing in a man. But then again, though he was arrogant, he hadn't looked down on her. He had been kind and caring, willing to help and willing to comfort. He was also handsome and her body had certainly reacted to him. But more important than all those traits combined, he had become a friend.

Still she resisted. Her husband had died just a year ago and she had only known Hilt for two days. In answer, her vision shifted again. She saw Hilt's life from the beginning. Watched his birth, his childhood. Saw his loves and losses. Saw every decision he made, both the good and the bad, the smart and the stupid. Oh there were so many stupid ones and yet, through it all, he was exactly the man she thought him to be.

Her vision brought her back to the present. Hilt was nearly at the stair. He was fighting strong, but that fight would end soon, one way or the other.

It was time for her to decide. Live or die?

She no longer wanted to die, but . . .

Beth tried to scan back over the possible paths ahead of her, but the vision began to fade. She raced back into Hilt's future, looking at the choices he faced, but she only had one last glimpse before it disappeared all together. She had been shown all she was meant to see. One thing was clear. Hilt needed her.

Beth made her choice. She rolled of the altar and as she stood, her foot landed on something soft.

"*Hurts!*" "*Hungry.*" "*Dance! Dance!*"

"Beth!" Hilt shouted and sent blades of air into the misshapen beasts with great swipes of his swords.

The guardians fell to pieces, but more came out of the caves towards him. The bodies of the beasts he slew sunk into the ground and he wondered if they weren't just reassembling in some cavern below and coming back for more.

He glanced to his left and saw Yntri slice one of the guardians in two. He had run out of arrows a while back, but now his bow had become a sword in his hands, as sharp as any steel blade. The elf attacked with fluidity and grace, as good as the best academy swordsmen. The white sap covering his body acted as armor, resisting the attacks of claw and beak.

"Beth!" he shouted again and spun, cleaving more beasts. Their weak points were the large mouths in the center of their torsos. When he cut off heads or appendages, they seemed to keep coming, but if he struck them across the middle, they went down pretty easy. If only there weren't so many.

"*Ancient one.*" "*EAT!*" "*Mine!*"

Where was she? If not for their constant cries of 'witch' he would be sure she was dead. But more than that, there was something in his heart that told him she wasn't. "Beth!"

Then he saw it arcing down from the cliff face; a long hand-carved stair. "Yntri! There, ahead!"

The elf was sprinting towards a large bear-like guardian with tentacles for arms. He also had discovered their weakness, for he dove into the open mouth on its chest, and sliced his way out the other side. As it fell to the ground with a great shower of blood, he clicked, pointing upward.

Hilt's eyes followed his finger towards the top of the cliff. There was an eerie glow emanating up there and he didn't like it. He ran for the stairs.

"Away." "Away." "Away."

The guardians howled in unison and poured out of the caves in greater numbers, packing the space between Hilt and the stair.

"Away." "Away." "Die."

Hilt refused to be cowed. He called out for Beth and unleashed his fury upon them, blades of air cutting the beasts down two, three at a time. They howled in protest and he redoubled his efforts. Beasts fell. Trees fell. There was only one important thing. He had to reach her. This was his quest. This was the responsibility placed on him by the Prophet. He was to see her to the top alive and if she was already up there, he intended to bring her back down alive.

Slowly he realized that their numbers were decreasing. The discarded hunks of their bodies were sinking into the earth, but they were not being replaced. He watched them slinking back to their hiding places.

"Enough." "Stop." "Hungy." "Witch!"

"Hah! Giving up?" He headed towards the caves. What if they had taken her in there? "Beth!"

"Hilt!"

He turned back and saw Beth approaching from the foot of the stair. She had an almost ethereal glow about her and a satisfied smile on her face.

"Beth!" he shouted. "Hurry to me before the beasts return!"

"They won't bother us any longer," Beth said calmly. She walked up and linked her arm in his.

"*Hungry*." *So hungry*." "*The pain*!" "*Named one*."

"Hush!" she spat, scowling over her shoulder and the voices quieted again.

Hilt's eyes widened and he looked at her in puzzlement. "Are you okay?"

"Yes, I am fine," she said and laid her head on his shoulder. "Let's go back down this mountain. You have a mission to finish."

Yntri padded over to them, covered in blood head to toe, but otherwise unharmed. He was using his Jharro bow to scrape the blood off his arms, but froze when he saw Beth leaning her head on Hilt's shoulder. He cocked his head at them quizzically and clicked out a question.

Hilt shrugged helplessly. "I don't know what's going on, Yntri." He wiped his swords clean on the body of the dissolving beast next to him and sheathed them, then gently pried Beth from his arm and held her away at arm's length. "Beth, what happened?"

She narrowed her eyes at him. "You would have died if I hadn't come back down, you know. These monsters are here to keep people like you away."

"Surely not," Hilt said with a grin. "These guardians weren't so-. Wait, people like me? Why?"

"The stair beyond is not for you," she explained.

"You made it to the top, didn't you?" Hilt's eyes followed the stairs as they ascended to the peak. What had she found up there? He took a step forward. Large dark shapes stirred again in the shadows at the stairs' base.

Beth placed a hand on his arm. "Don't be tempted, Hilt. There really is nothing for you up there."

Hilt's hands gripped his swords, but when he looked back to her, something in her eyes convinced him. He nodded and let go. "Very well. Did you find what you were looking for?"

"I did. And Yntri . . ." She lifted a small leather pouch. "I nearly tripped over this on the way down. I think it's for you."

Yntri clicked a question as he walked forward. She let the pouch drop into his hand. When he opened it up, his ancient eyes opened wide and he barked out an excited laugh. He reached inside and pulled out a handful of what looked like gray pebbles. He touched one to the side of his Jharro bow and the pebble stuck in place. Then it slowly sank into the wood. He whistled and jumped up and down in excitement. He poured the pebbles back into the pouch and tucked it into his knapsack.

Yntri threw his arms around her, clicking in gratitude. She hugged him back, heedless of the blood and Jharro sap that now clung to the front of her clothing. "Is this what you were searching for?"

Yntri nodded and clicked before embracing her again.

Hilt smiled, happy for both of them. If only his journey had ended with such a satisfying conclusion. Sure, he had gotten the chance to fight the guardians, but he didn't feel like he had truly beaten them. His mind wandered back to the troll behemoth in the caves deep below. Fighting the guardians had given him a few ideas on how to kill it.

"Hilt," Beth said sweetly, interrupting his thoughts. "Will you pry Yntri off of me please, before I club him to death?"

"I think he's fallen asleep," Hilt said. The elf's head was nestled against her chest and his eyes were closed. Soft snoring sounds buzzed from his nose.

"I know you don't sleep, elf!" Beth snapped, knocking him upside the head with the flat of her palm. "Now get off me or I'm taking that bag of seeds back to the top of this mountain and leaving them there!"

Yntri didn't pull away, but instead snuggled in even closer. Beth's face went red and she swung back a fist, but Hilt grabbed her wrist.

"I'm serious. He is asleep," he said with a chuckle.

"Who sleeps like that?" Beth said incredulously. "Just standing there leaning on a person's . . . chest?"

"That's how his people sleep." Hilt insisted. "Not wrapped around a person usually, but up in the Jharro trees, clutching a branch."

She didn't quite believe him, but then again, the old elf did look peaceful, even if he was filthy.

"He has been searching for those seeds for a long time and I haven't seen him sleep once while on this trip," Hilt said with an amused smile. "And you should have seen him fighting back there. He should be tired."

"Well he's not sleeping on me," Beth said, reaching around her back trying to work his fingers loose. His grip was tight. "Just help me pry him off . . . please?"

Hilt walked behind her and with great effort, pulled the elf's hands free. Beth slipped out of his grasp and left Hilt holding Yntri's hand apart while the elf stood, still very much asleep. Hilt sighed and hoisted the elf over his back. As soon as he had him in position, Yntri's arms and legs wrapped around him, latching on tight.

He looked back at Beth, he found her watching him with her head cocked. "I know. I look quite ridiculous."

"It's not that," she said. "You don't look too satisfied with the end of our journey."

"No, it's not that. I am quite happy for the both of you. You've found your answers. It's just . . . we have a long way down and I have got to be nearly as tired as Yntri."

"Oh, I was going to tell you," Beth said. "There's something else I learned at the top of those stairs. There is a much easier path along the back side of the mountain. We took the hard way up."

"Ah," Hilt said and his shoulders slumped. "That should make me feel better, but somehow it doesn't."

"I found an answer for you too," she said, linking her arm back in his. She turned him away from the stair.

"Oh really?" he asked, eyebrows raised in interest.

"Remember yesterday when you told me that once you

have reached the peak, there is nowhere to go but down?" Hilt nodded and she shook her head. "You were wrong."

"Was I?" he asked.

"Yes, Hilt. You see, this is a big world. There is always another mountain to climb."

He thought about it for a moment, then gave her a knowing glance. "You saw a lot more up there, didn't you?"

She gave him a coy smile and led back towards the ridge line. "Why yes I did, Sir Hilt."

They headed out of the trees, Hilt expecting her to elaborate. But she didn't. They hiked back down the ridgeline and Hilt was glad that Yntri was such a light old elf. When they arrived back at the boulder that was the source of the hot spring, Beth showed him the narrow trail that led down the back side of the mountain.

"Beth," Hilt said. "Aren't you going to tell me what you saw?"

"Perhaps," Beth replied and as they walked down the narrow path, she rested her head on his shoulder again. "But some revelations are best saved for later."

The following is a preview of The Bowl of Souls Book Four:

The WAR of STARDEON

Coming 2013

Author Note

This preview will contain some spoilers for those of you who have not read the first three books. I don't believe that there is any information contained in this section that will ruin your enjoyment of the other books. But nonetheless I feel compelled to warn you ahead of time. As always, thank you for reading and if you like what you read, please tell your friends.

Trevor H. Cooley

THE WAR OF STARDEON
PROLOGUE

"Lord Protector Vriil behind this siege? Hmph, preposterous," said a man Willum had never seen before. The man stood with arms folded and spoke with calm measure but his round face had grown quite red. It was not a good look for him. His nose had been bulbous and dark when Willum had started his report and now it looked positively purple.

"This is what my father said, yes," Willum replied. He looked around the Battle Academy council table but no one leapt to his defense. The reason he had been brought in was to retell his story for the members of the newly assembled War Council. He hadn't expected to be interrogated. The first time he had told the council of his father's warning, the table had been supportive and full of questions. This time they just sat quietly and listened. Even Tad the Cunning said nothing. He was watching the stranger's reaction over steepled fingers, his elbows resting on the council table.

The War Council was put into effect whenever the academy came under siege. The members were comprised of the leaders from the different factions held within the academy's walls. The members included the regular Battle Academy council, the Training School Council, and Demon Jenn, the mayor of Reneul.

"Hearsay. And it comes from a man living in another kingdom. That is what the Queen would say if I told her this rubbish," the stranger said. He was short and stocky and wore an expensive puffy shirt of silken brocade with collar and cuffs made of flowing lace. Willum thought the outfit looked itchy. Perhaps the man was a noble or merchant of some sort, but that didn't explain why everyone was listening to him.

The stranger sat down in his chair and leaned back, placing his hands behind his head. "Why are we even considering these accusations?"

"Master Coal is a named wizard and a friend of the academy," said Hugh the Shadow, head of the academy's Assassin Guild. "We have no reason to doubt his word." Hugh gave Willum a pointed look as he spoke and Willum felt his face flush with embarrassment. The council hadn't exactly been happy with him when he had revealed his father's identity. He had been keeping it a secret, determined not to let Coal's status be part of the factor determining his entrance into the academy. He had wanted to do it on his own. Hiding the identity of one's father wasn't uncommon, but it was frowned upon, especially hiding it from the council. Willum was just glad that they didn't know the identity of his birth father. That would have complicated things greatly.

"And Master Coal has sworn witnesses to Ewzad Vriil's actions," said Sabre Vlad, head of the Swordwielder's Guild.

"Oh, right. The witnesses. An elf, a dwarf, and an ogre. An ogre? Please." Despite his nonchalance, the mystery man's nose was getting even purpler.

"There is also Sir Edge," Willum added. "He is the named warrior who was imprisoned by Ewzad Vriil for a time. He saw Ewzad Vriil use magic. He even saw him call an army of goblinoids to fight for him."

"More hearsay. Tales from a named warrior no one has ever heard of, talking about a battle in the Lord Protector's keep that supposedly released hundreds of prisoners and yet no one has heard of the incident!" There was definite anger in his voice now and he was scowling. A vein throbbed on the man's temple and his nose had become so engorged Willum feared it might burst.

"What I think would help is if you could show us the letter in your father's hand," said Demon Jenn. "Or perhaps you could produce some kind of signed statement from the witnesses?" Jenn was an academy graduate, as most of the mayors of Reneul had been over the years. She had earned her name on the battlefield and was well respected, but the years had not been kind to her. Her face had been disfigured by a goblin dagger while protecting a caravan in her youth and as she had aged, the scar had shrunken and puckered, leaving one lip pulled upward in a permanent sneer.

"I am sorry, ma'am. That isn't possible," Willum said. "My-."

"Hmph! Again, the lack of proof." the stranger said. "I still don't see why we are listening to this."

"This information didn't come by letter," Tad the Cunning said, speaking up for the first time since Willum had entered the room. His eyes remained on the fancily dressed man as he spoke, "Willum, please explain to everyone how you received your father's message."

"Of course, sir."

Willum couldn't tell them of the true nature of the bond he had with Coal. Bonding magic was rare and unknown to most of the wizard community and the rest of the world was completely ignorant of its existence. Instead, he recited the story Coal had concocted the first time he had Willum pass a message on to the council.

"When I left home, my father wanted to be able to keep in contact with me, so he used a spell to set up a . . . mental connection. Even though he is very far away, if we are both concentrating, we can communicate to each other with our minds. It's not easy. I-I can usually only accomplish it at night, sir. When I am laying in my bed after all my tasks are complete, for instance."

The story wouldn't have held up if a wizard had been in the room. As far as Willum knew, no such spell existed within the realm of elemental magic. There were objects enchanted to carry people or items over long distances, but to send one's thoughts was a more difficult task. Only spiritual magic could accomplish that.

The man smirked and opened his mouth to retort, but Tad spoke first.

"I have a piece of evidence to back up his claim." He picked up a scroll and slid it over to Demon Jenn. "This scroll arrived from the Mage School not long before the attack. They had received a similar communication from Master Coal and urged us to heed his warnings. They vouch for his words and his methods."

The mayor opened the scroll and nodded appreciatively. For a woman that made her name in battle, she seemed to put a lot of trust in paperwork. "This is signed by Master Latva himself." She directed her gaze to the stranger. "This eases my mind."

"So one wizard vouches for another? What does that change? Let me see that. Do they include any new evidence to support his claims?" The man snatched the scroll away from her and poured over it with his eyes.

Tad cleared his throat. "You are ignoring another fact. Many of Master Coal's claims have already proven true. His witnesses knew of the army amassing in the mountains. He warned us that an attack could be coming. If he had not warned us through his connection with his son, we may have been caught unawares."

Willum's shoulders sank in relief. Finally Tad was backing him up. The tension in the room had been giving him a headache.

The man stood, his face twisted in anger, more purple than ever. He paused and closed his eyes for a moment. His shoulders quivered briefly and he blinked a few times before clearing his throat. He raised one shaking hand and smoothed back his thinning hair. He saw everyone staring and smiled apologetically before sitting down. Much of the extra color had drained from his face.

"Are you okay?" Tad asked. "Can we get you some water or something?"

"No, I'm fine, fine. Uh, your point is well taken, Tad. However, just because this Master Coal was right about the invasion does not mean that his witnesses are right about everything else. A man can be right in some cases and wrong in others. I for one still refuse to believe that Lord Protector Vriil had anything to do with this attack. I will need to see better evidence than this if I am to send a message warning the queen."

"I understand your position." Tad's eyes left the man and moved to Willum. "Has your father told you anything new to report, Willum?"

Willum swallowed. He was already dreading the stranger's reaction to his news. "Yes, he has gathered a small band of . . . warriors and along with Sir Edge is travelling here to help in whatever way he can. As they began their journey, they were attacked by several of Ewzad Vriil's altered beasts. They lost one of their number but were able to defeat the beasts and have since continued on their way."

"And when was this?" Tad asked.

"Two days ago, sir."

"Beasts made by the Lord Protector? Surely you don't expect us to believe- . . . Never mind," the stranger said with a shake of his head. The color was flooding his face again and his voice was loaded with sarcasm as he asked, "Well, why don't you describe these horrible creatures for us?"

Willum swallowed. He knew that his description would sound outlandish to say the least. "There was an armored orc that spat acid, a large plant-like beast with razor sharp whips, and a huge red beast that flew like a dragon and radiated heat from its very skin. Father called it a bandham."

The stranger laughed in derision, though to Willum, it seemed that his eyes weren't laughing. They were watching him with calculating intensity. Thankfully no one else in the room found it funny.

"Thank you, Willum, son of Coal," Tad said with a nod. "Please keep the council informed of any new developments." He looked back to the rest of the council. "I believe Stout Harley has a report on our current supply situation. If you will excuse me for a moment?"

Tad smiled and stood from his chair. He nudged Willum on his way to the back of the chamber and Willum followed him out the rear door of the council hall.

Willum followed Tad down a hallway and passed several rooms that he didn't know the purpose of. He knew that the rear of the building contained the personal apartments of the council members but had never been in this part of the building. They walked down some stairs and headed down a dimly lit corridor. At the second junction, Tad stopped and grabbed Willum's shoulder. He kept his voice low.

"I am sorry I had to put you through that."

"Who was that man?" Willum asked, relieved that his teacher was acting more like normal.

"He is Dann Doudy, the new Dremald representative to the academy."

"The new representative? What happened to Proud Harold?" Willum asked. Harold had been the Dremald representative on the council for over a decade. He was a jovial man and well liked by the students. When King Andre had died and his sister Elise had been crowned, Harold had been summoned back to Dremald along with the rest of the Dremald troops that were usually assigned to the academy.

"I don't know and that concerns me. This . . . Dann Doudy, showed up the evening before the attack. He had papers from the queen announcing him as Harold's replacement. He says Harold had grown weary of his duties and wanted to retire."

Willum's brow knit in concern. If his father's suspicions about the situation in Dremald were correct, something bad may have happened to Harold. "What do you know about this new representative?"

Tad frowned. "Not much. He is a minor noble. The Doudy family has been in Dremaldria for generations, but why the queen would choose him is a mystery. She didn't list any of his qualifications."

"I understand," Willum said. Tad's behavior in the conference room was making sense now. He had been watching the man's response to his father's warning to gauge his reaction. "So do you think he was sent here to keep an eye on us?"

"If he was sent here by Ewzad Vriil as a spy, he isn't a very effective one." He stroked his chin. "He definitely hasn't been trying to make any friends since he arrived. No spy worth his spit would have acted so bothered by our information. His actions were so bizarre it makes me wonder if he was acting the avid Vriil supporter to throw us off. A pretty clever ploy, I must say. I'm interested to see what Hugh thought of his act."

"And what if he is reporting information to the enemy?" Willum asked. "He will be in every council meeting. He could tell the enemy how many men we have, how they men are positioned, what our food supplies are . . ."

Tad patted his shoulder. "Good. You are thinking this through. I can tell you have been paying attention in my class. But don't worry. I have archers posted on the wall looking for birds. We are watching any possible form of communication. We are safe unless he was somehow able to get out of the academy, but we are surrounded by tens of thousands of goblinoids, and we have soldiers at every possible exit. There is no way he is sneaking out."

"Good to know, sir." Willum said with relief.

"Unless, you think . . . Could Ewzad Vriil possibly use a spell like your father has been using to communicate with you?"

Willum swallowed. "I don't think so. It is a spell of my father's own creation." But what if he could? Coal had told him that Ewzad Vriil had the rings of Stardeon and that those rings used spiritual magic. What if Ewzad Vriil had found a way to make a mental connection with this noble? He would have to ask Coal later that night through the bond.

There was a sound down the corridor and Tad looked to make sure that no one was coming. "Now you must keep this conversation to yourself. I do not want doubts about our new representative being passed through the students. They have enough to worry about. The only reason I told you about my concerns is that I need you to pass them on to your father. See if he has any information about Dann Doudy. Get his opinion. And one other thing . . ." He looked into Willum's eyes. "I want you reporting directly to me from now on. He is our only pair of eyes outside the wall right now. Any new information your father tells you, bring it to my attention. No matter how small, you understand? Tell no one else."

Willum nodded, "But-."

"I mean no one. Don't even tell the other council members.

Report to me only. I don't plan on bringing you back before the council unless it is absolutely necessary."

"Yes sir," Willum replied. Was Tad worried about the loyalty of the other academy teachers?

"Good. Now it is time I returned to the council. You should go about your duties." Tad gave him a confident smile. "Don't worry too much about our new representative. We are watching him."

"Of course, sir."

"Just head down the corridor to the left and you'll reach the entrance."

"Thank you, sir."

Tad the Cunning turned and walked back towards the council hall and Willum turned up the joining corridor as instructed. After a short distance, it opened into the long high-ceilinged foyer at the front of the building. As Willum walked towards the outer doors, he looked at the tapestries depicting the glorious battles of the academy's past and wondered if the current siege would be depicted on these walls some day. He supposed it would, if they survived.

When he reached the doors he nodded to the two guards at their posts on either side of the doors. He took a deep breath before grasping the handles.

"Going out's always the hard part, ain't it, Willum?" said one of the guards.

"Yeah, Zhed." he said. "It's nice and quiet in here."

The architect that had designed the council building had put it together so that all sound from outside was cut out. His teacher had told the class that the effect was caused by the cunning way the blocks of stone had been put together, but Willum was pretty sure he had a wizard's help. Whatever the case, it was effective.

The other guard snorted. "Quiet? I call it boring. I'd rather be on the wall looking down at the goblinoids. It's all I can do to keep from falling asleep."

Willum shrugged. "I would suggest you enjoy the quiet

while you can."

He pushed open the doors and walked out into a wave of sound. The academy was packed with people and the high walls caused even small sounds to echo. Students were training, smiths pounding away on anvils, citizens rushing back and forth on errands, shouting to each other, and behind it all was the low drone of the goblinoid army surrounding them.

The Dremaldrian Battle Academy usually had around two thousand students and close to five hundred faculty and graduates waiting for jobs. When the incoming attack had been confirmed, the Training School had been halted and all trainees brought inside. Reneul was evacuated. Anyone who wanted to stay behind was brought inside the academy walls. Now there were over four thousand people crammed inside.

The dorms and outbuildings were overflowing. Cots and tents had been set up in the yards. Even many of the seldom-used tunnels underneath the academy had been opened up for people to sleep in. The council building was the only structure not packed with people.

Willum hurried along, weaving his way along the congested pathways that crisscrossed the grounds. He was late for his shift on the academy wall. This time of day he was supposed to be on the northeast corner. So far the enemy hadn't attacked and were content to marshal their forces and more goblinoids joined their ranks from the mountains every day. The faculty switched up shifts a few times a day to keep the students alert. Each wall had its own perils to watch for. It seemed that in order to stave off infighting, the army had been split into racial groups.

The eastern wall looked out over the Training School grounds where the gorcs were camped. The training tents still stood, along with the barracks and marketplace and several small arenas. When on watch there, Willum could hear the gorcs using them. Fighting for sport seemed to be their favorite form of entertainment.

The north wall overlooked the Scralag Hills, which had been mostly overtaken by giants and ogre tribes. They seemed to make a game of getting as close to the wall as they dared and throwing jagged rocks. The students and graduates on the wall shot arrows to keep them at a safe distance and most of their throws fell short, but every once in a while one would clear the top. The large beasts roared and hollered when one of their rocks made it over. Luckily, there had only been a few injuries so far.

The western wall looked out over what would once have been empty farmland, but was now covered in goblins. They were the most unruly bunch, always yelling and hollering, making obscene gestures and fighting amongst each other. They were more a source of entertainment than a source for concern.

The southern wall shift was the trickiest. It overlooked the main city of Reneul which was full of buildings for the enemy to hide in. The east half of the city, which included the huge academy arena and the majority of the homes had been taken over by orcs. They seemed the most organized part of the army, always marching around in units and busily taking buildings apart to build siege engines. In the short time since the siege had begun, they already had several catapults, battering rams and trebuchets.

Western Reneul had been overtaken by trolls and other monsters. Strangely, they seemed to mill about peacefully, only screeching and attacking when the orcs threw them food. At night, while the other parts of the army were aglow with torches and camp fires, western Reneul would be scattered with the glow of yellow and green moonrat eyes. The unsettling sound of their chittering moans made night on the southwestern wall the most dreaded shift on the wall.

Willum groaned as he approached the duty desk at the base of the wall. Roobin was in charge of check-in again. Roobin wasn't a bad guy; he was good-natured most of the time and not bad with a sword, but he had recently graduated and loved giving Willum a hard time about it.

"Willum, son of Coal, reporting for duty."

"Oh, the mighty son of Coal, eh?" Roobin chuckled, though it was only a few short weeks ago that he had been known as Roobin, son of Roobin the Knuckle.

"Just sign me in, okay?"

"You are kind of late, aren't you? Whoo, students should not be tardy." Roobin dipped his quill and looked down at the log-in sheet. His smirk faded. "Lucky you. Go on to station twenty eight. I guess I don't have to report you."

"You were gonna report me?" Willum said in disbelief.

"Of course, except that it says here that Tad called you away. So you have an excuse."

"Oh, so it's just 'Tad' now, is it?" Willum said, getting in a jab of his own. "Just because you have graduated, you two are on a first name basis? Should I be calling you, 'Roobin, the Well Connected' now?"

Roobin's eyes narrowed. "Shut up, Willum. Just go on up. You're relieving Swen, son of Rolf, the Fletcher."

"Yes sir!" Willum said with a salute, and grabbed a bow and quiver from the rack next to the stairs. Some students carried around their own bows, but that wasn't Willum's forte. He was okay with a bow, but his specialty was his scythe and throwing daggers.

He headed up the stairs pleased with the irritation on Roobin's face, but as he reached the top of the wall, his pleasure faded. A mix of his fellow students and academy graduates lined the walls looking down at the massive army that sprawled below. The dull roar of the enemy was much louder up here. It was rough and rhythmic.

Willum was careful not to touch anyone as he walked to his station. The top of the wall was wide enough for three men to walk side by side and there was an abdomen high barrier on either side, but no matter how many shifts he took, it always made him nervous if someone brushed against him while he was at the edge.

Swen was at post twenty eight, bending over the edge and staring down unconcerned at the height. Swen was a tall man, maybe six foot four and the wall's edge only came up to his waist. Though he was only a few years older than Willum, his face was angular and weathered, with wrinkles at the corners of his eyes from squinting in the sun. He was also the best archery student the academy had seen in decades. Swen made all his own arrows and the other students had started calling him Swen the Feather. Willum thought the name was going to stick.

"Swen I'm here," he said. "Sorry, but Tad the Cunning called me away for a while."

"Yeah, that's fine." The tall man barely gave him a glance as he spoke. His eyes were focused on the army below. "I've been up here for eight straight hours, what's another one or two?"

"What's the problem?" Willum looked down, trying to see what was bothering the man. The base of the wall was clear of enemies for a good two hundred yards on this side of the school as the army tried to keep out of shooting distance. But there was one group of goblinoids that were gathered in a bit closer than the others. They were the chanters. There were groups of them all around the wall. A mixed group of orcs, gorcs, and goblins sat cross-legged on the ground, slightly swaying back and forth, chanting loudly. They had been at it for days. Every once in a while one of them would pass out and be dragged away, but they were always replaced.

"I don't like the sound of that grunting down there," Swen said, his voice a low monotone.

"Yeah, it gives me the shivers."

"What do you think they are doing?" Swen asked.

Willum had asked Coal the same question the night before. He had relayed his memory of the chant and had Coal pass it on to Bettie. Her answer had been unsettling.

"They're chanting a prayer to the Dark Prophet," Willum said. "They ask him to bring the wall down."

"Oh." Swen's face paled. The big man lifted his massive bow and pulled a long arrow from his quiver. Swen's bow was nearly as tall as Willum and as thick as his forearm. Swen had named it Windy. It had been reinforced with runes to keep it from weathering or cracking and most of the other students couldn't even string it, much less shoot with it. Even Mad Jon, the archery teacher, had difficulty with firing it.

"Be careful," Willum said. "You know the rules. We aren't supposed to waste any arrows. Only fire if they come in range."

Swen looked at him in surprise. "Have you ever known me to miss?" He focused on the group chanting below. "I figure the one with the black feathers on his armor is the leader."

Willum peered down and located the orc Swen spoke of. It wore some kind of headdress bristling with something like feathers and walked among the rows of chanting orcs waving its arms about as if to encourage them to chant louder. "He does look the most energetic."

Swen pulled the arrow back to his ear, the muscles on his arms taught with the strain.

"It'll just . . . make it." Swen grunted. Willum heard the wood creak as he gave it an extra pull. Swen sucked in, then slowly released his breath as he fired.

Willum saw the arrow arc out, but lost track of it for most of the distance until he saw the black-feathered orc squirm and squeal. The arrow had it struck it in the belly. The chanting stopped and the goblinoids pointed urgently at the top of the wall. Swen waved. Several of them grabbed their dying leader and they retreated back another fifty yards.

"Great shot!" Willum said.

"Hit it in the belly," Swen said with a slight frown. "I was aiming for its neck."

"Can you hit another one?" Willum asked. They were startled now. If another went down, they might not be able to chant so freely.

Swen shook his head. "Just out of range."

"Well I'm here now. You can go rest if you want," Willum said. "Unless you want to move further along the wall and see if you can disperse some more chanters."

The tall man smiled. "Good idea." He pulled another arrow from his quiver and walked down the wall looking for more targets.

Willum took his place and looked down at the mass of beasts below. A cool breeze blew and the smell that wafted up was horrible. The air on this side of the academy used to smell of tilled earth and pine trees. Now it stank of beasts and filth and cook fires mixed with an underlying rot.

Willum shuddered. It was hard to believe that this was all the work of his uncle.

CPSIA information can be obtained
at www.ICGtesting.com
Printed in the USA
LVOW01s0009230716
497463LV00010B/429/P

9 781484 069127